C0-AMS-022

HAMLET

– novel –

PAUL ILLIDGE

Creber Monde

In memory of Stephen Eby 1964-1993

Copyright © 2005 Paul Illidge

All rights reserved. No portion of this book, with the exception of brief extracts for the purpose of literary or scholarly review, may be reproduced in any form without the permission of the publisher.

Caution: This version of *Hamlet* is fully protected under the copyright laws of Canada and all other countries of The Copyright Union, and is subject to royalty. Unauthorized use of the text is expressly forbidden. Rights to produce, film or record, in whole or in part, in any medium or in any language, by any group, amateur or professional, are retained by the author.

Published by Creber Monde Entier
265 Port Union, 15-532
Toronto, ON M1C 4Z7 Canada
(416) 286-3988 1-866-631-4440 toll free
www.crebermonde.com
publisher@crebermonde.com

Distributed by Independent Publishers Group
814 North Franklin Street
Chicago, Illinois 60610 USA
(312) 337-0747 (312) 337-5985 fax
www.ipgbook.com
frontdesk@ipgbook.com

Design by Derek Chung Tiam Fook
Communications by JAG Business Services Inc.
Printed and bound in Canada by Hignell Book Printing, Winnipeg, Manitoba

Second Printing August 2006

Library and Archives Canada Cataloguing in Publication

Illidge, Paul
Hamlet / prose translation by Paul Illidge.

(The Shakespeare novels)
ISBN 0-9686347-3-7

I. Title. II. Series: Illidge, Paul. Shakespeare novels.

PR2878.H35I45 2005 C813'.54 C2005-901591-8

HAMLET

Text of the First Folio 1623

Characters

Hamlet	*Prince of Denmark*
King Claudius	*King of Denmark, Hamlet's uncle*
Ghost	*Hamlet's father, former King of Denmark*
Queen Gertrude	*Hamlet's mother, now wife of Claudius*
Polonius	*councillor to the Danish State*
Laertes	*son of Polonius*
Ophelia	*daughter of Polonius*
Horatio	*university friend and confidant of Hamlet*

Rosencrantz
Guildenstern — *courtiers, boyhood friends of Hamlet*

Fortinbras — *Prince of Norway*

Voltemand
Cornelius — *councillors of State, ambassadors to Norway*

Marcellus
Barnardo — *members of the King's guard*
Francisco

Osric	*a foppish courtier*
Reynaldo	*servant of Polonius*
Players	
Gentleman	*of the court*
Priest	
Gravedigger	
Partner	*to the gravedigger*
Captain	*in Fortinbras's army*
English Ambassadors	

Lords, Ladies, Soldiers, Sailors, Messengers, Attendants

Late in the 16th century, on a platform atop the walls of Elsinore Castle in Denmark, a guard named Francisco is on night duty when he suddenly hears someone coming through the darkness.

"Who's there?" a man's voice calls.

"You tell me first!" Francisco replies, readying his poleax. "Show your face!"

"Long live the King!" the voice shouts back.

"Barnardo?" Francisco soon makes out the face of his fellow guard.

"You're here early tonight," Francisco remarks, relaxing his weapon.

"It's already midnight. Why don't you go to bed."

Francisco shrugs, relieved. "Thanks. I could use a break. It's freezing up here. Lonely too."

"Any trouble?"

"No. It's been quiet."

"Well, good night. If you see Horatio and Marcellus, tell them I'll be waiting."

"Of course – hang on," Francisco says in a low voice. "Who's there?" he calls.

"Friends!" a voice answers in the darkness.

"Subjects of the King of Denmark, like you!" adds another voice. "Barnardo?"

"Marcellus – over here! Is Horatio with you?"

"A piece of him," Horatio offers obscurely, as if here in body more than in spirit.

After bidding goodnight to the departing Francisco, he and Marcellus greet Barnardo as he takes up his post.

Waiting till he's sure Francisco is gone, Marcellus asks if "the thing" has appeared again.

"No, not yet," Barnardo says uneasily.

Horatio chuckles quietly.

"What's wrong?" Barnardo asks.

"Horatio says it's a figment of our imagination," Marcellus explains. "He doesn't believe we've seen it, so I asked him to come along tonight. Maybe he can try making contact with it."

"Come on, Marcellus," Horatio teases.

"Sit down and we'll tell you how it happens."

"How a ghost just *happens* to appear –"

"Like I told you before, a little after the one o'clock bell sounded last night –"

"Things were just like they are right now –"

"Shhh!" Marcellus whispers. "Be quiet!"

"What?"

The three men squint into the darkness along the platform. "There it is!" Marcellus shouts, pointing across the way.

"It's the ghost of the dead King!"

"You know about these things, Horatio – speak to it!"

"Doesn't it look exactly like the dead King?" Barnardo cries.

"So much like him it's disturbing," Horatio says.

"It wants us to speak to it," Marcellus insists.

"Go on Horatio!"

Amazed, Horatio advances toward the hovering apparition. "Why have you come here tonight? And why are you dressed in the armor of our dead King?"

The ghostly presence shimmers in silence.

"Tell me what you're doing here!" Horatio demands more firmly.

"It looks offended," Marcellus observes.

"It's going away!" cries Barnardo.

"Stop! Answer my question!" Horatio calls.

But the ghost vanishes into the darkness.

"What's wrong?" Barnardo asks Horatio. "Your face is pale and you're shaking all over."

Horatio continues staring into the darkness. "I wouldn't believe it if I hadn't seen it with my own eyes," he says, shivering.

"You see? We weren't just imagining things."

"It was the spitting image of the King," Barnardo declares.

"As you are of yourself," Horatio admits. "It's strange he had on the identical armour the King wore fighting Norway just before he died. Even the angry frown on his face was the same."

"This makes three times it's come out while we were on duty," Marcellus remarks. "Three times!"

Horatio considers what Marcellus has just said with what he himself has just seen. "It's impossible to be certain, but I think it could mean Denmark's in store for some kind of trouble."

Marcellus nods. "The kind of trouble that has us on watch every night now. It's like we're preparing for war all over again – forging cannons, buying guns on the foreign market. The shipbuilders are working seven days a week, 24 hours a day." He shakes his head in frustration. "I wish somebody could tell me what's going on...."

The minutes pass slowly, the three men sitting on the castle ramparts in the cold night air, unsettled by what they've seen, unsure whether the ghostly figure will reappear as the night wears on.

With time to ruminate on what Marcellus has said about Denmark readying itself for a military campaign, Horatio finally offers a possible explanation. He believes it's got something to do with Prince Fortinbras, the son of Norway's former King, who wagered parts of his kingdom in a dispute with King Hamlet of Denmark. Since Fortinbras lost, he had to forfeit his lands, but now the young prince, his son, is bent on revenge. The rumor is that he's been putting together an army made up of criminals and outcasts who fight for pay, even if it's no more than free meals. This Fortinbras believes the confiscated lands are rightly his, although if his father had won the war he would have taken over sections of Hamlet's Danish kingdom. In any event, the country's getting ready for the Norwegians to attack.

"Maybe the dead King has come back to warn us then," Barnardo surmises.

"Either that, or something worse," Horatio adds, the implication being an impending civil war in Denmark. "Don't forget," he continues, "in the days of imperial Rome, just before Julius Caesar was assassinated, they say the dead rose up from their graves and wandered the streets in their burial sheets. There were other omens too, like shooting stars and lunar eclipses every night, and some claim the morning dew actually had a red tinge to it – wait! Here it comes again!"

Horatio and the two guards jump to their feet. "Wait!" Horatio calls and runs after the ghost. "If you have the ability, speak to me! Tell me if there is something I can do to ease your burden! If there's impending trouble in the kingdom we could somehow avoid! Please, tell me spirit!" He and the two guards are trying to corral the elusive apparition, when a rooster begins to crow.

"Shall I hit it with my spear?" Marcellus cries.

"It's over here!" Barnardo shouts.

"No, it's here!" Horatio yells from behind him.

"It's gone," Marcellus points out in frustration. "We shouldn't have been so aggressive with it. It's invulnerable to anything we could do."

"As soon as the cock began to crow it just vanished," Barnardo observes.

"Like it was being summoned elsewhere," Horatio remarks. "I've heard that the rooster when it announces morning's arrival with its shrill cry is actually warning wandering spirits, wherever they roam, to hurry back into hiding; which is exactly what happened just now."

"True, it faded away as soon as the rooster crowed," Marcellus says. "You know," he remarks, "some people say that just before Christmas the rooster sings all night long, so that no spirit dares show itself, nothing unwholesome fouls the night air, the planets exert no evil influence, no fairy plays tricks, and no witch can cast spells, because it's such a holy and sacred time of year."

"I've heard that as well," Horatio says, "and I half believe it. But look there, the morning in its russet red cloak is advancing across the dew-covered eastern hills. Our watch is over." He looks to Barnardo and Marcellus. "I suggest we let Prince Hamlet know what we've seen tonight. I have a feeling this spirit, which wouldn't speak to us, will make an effort to communicate with him. As friends, I think it's our duty to tell him, wouldn't you agree?"

"No question," Marcellus nods. "I know where we'll find him at this time of day."

The morning sky brightening behind them, the three men get to their feet and move off along the platform atop the castle walls.

Following a regal trumpet fanfare, Claudius, King of Denmark, sweeps into the throne room with Queen Gertrude, his Council of advisers (including Voltemand, Cornelius, Polonius and his son Laertes), an assortment of additional courtiers, and Hamlet, son of the previous King, dressed in black clothes.

"Though the memory of my dear brother Hamlet's death is still fresh," Claudius says, addressing the assembly, "and though as befits the passing of a monarch I have grieved deeply along with the whole kingdom, the time has come for good judgment to prevail so that we think of him wisely through our sorrow and remember that we must move on with our own lives. Therefore have I, my former sister-in-law, by imperial right my ruling partner in this divided state – with a sense of joyful defeat, mirth amid mourning, lament mixed with nuptial bliss, weighing delight and despair in equal balance – taken as my wife. For the advice and counsel so many of you have given us in freely supporting this decision, we offer you our thanks."

Personal matters dispensed with, Claudius turns his attention to state business. "As you know, Prince Fortinbras of neighboring Norway, assuming that the recent death of my brother King Hamlet has left us militarily weak and our country in a state of chaos, and believing that he now has us at a disadvantage, continues to pester us with messages demanding the surrender of those lands his father the King of Norway surrendered to our former King as part of an agreed upon peace settlement. That is his position. Our position, and the purpose of this meeting, is to share our response with you: we have written to the King of Norway, uncle of Prince Fortinbras, who, sick and bedridden now, is unaware of his nephew's actions, and we have requested he stop these proceedings against us – conscripting soldiers, drawing up battle plans and recruiting troops throughout Norway in preparation for war.

"Cornelius and Voltemand, we dispatch you to take this letter of greeting to the Norwegian King, authorizing you to negotiate with him on the basis of the articles included here. Farewell, and let your haste demonstrate your patriotic duty."

"In this as in all matters, you can rely on us," Cornelius and Voltemand reply, bowing obediently before the King.

"I have no doubt. A hearty farewell," Claudius says, dismissing them. "And now, Laertes, what's the news with you? I'm told there is something you want to discuss, something worthwhile I have no doubt. Don't be shy – the King is only too happy to oblige any reasonable request. What would you like, that would be mine to offer rather than yours to ask for? Bear in mind the head is as related to the heart, the hand to the mouth, as the throne of Denmark is to your father. What do you want?"

"My honored lord, your leave and blessing to return to France, from whence I dutifully came to celebrate your coronation. To be frank, that duty now done, I would like to go back if you would grant me your gracious permission to do so."

"What does your father say? Polonius? Does he have your permission?"

"He has managed to wring it out of me through persistent petitioning. In the end I finally – though I have to say reluctantly – consented. I beseech you to let him go, sire."

"Go ahead then, Laertes. Leave when the time is right, and make the most of your experience abroad." Laertes acknowledges the King with a polite bow, and departs.

"Now, my kinsman Hamlet," Claudius begins, turning to the Prince. "My nephew, as well as my son," he points out to the assembled nobles.

"So much more than kinsman, so much less than son," Hamlet mutters under his breath. If Claudius hears, he doesn't let on...

"Why won't the sun relinquish his clouds of mourning?"

"On the contrary, my lord. I'm in the sun much more than I should be."

"Dear Hamlet," the Queen suggests, "cease your somber brooding and look on the King as your friend. You can't keep your downcast eyes searching in the dust for your noble father forever. You know it is common; all living things die eventually, passing from this world to the next."

"Yes, madam, it is common."

"But it seems so personal to you."

"Seems, madam? No, it *is*. I don't know 'seems.' And it's not just the black cloak, good mother, or the funeral attire, the long and plaintive sighs, flowing tears, dejected looks, nor any form, mood or guise of grief that denotes my true feelings. These things indeed 'seem', being actions that a man might play; but I have that within which goes beyond show, that which is more than the appearance of sorrow."

"It is admirable and touching," the King says "that you mourn your father so conscientiously, Hamlet. But you realize of course that he lost his father, and your grandfather lost his father before that – it goes without saying that surviving family members are entitled to feel abject sorrow for a time, however wallowing obstinately over the loss borders on stubborn blasphemy, it's unmanly grief and it shows contempt for divine will, not to mention emotional weakness, an unstable mind, a naïve and foolish understanding; for what we know is inevitable, the most common of human experiences – why should we try to deny it, or let it affect us personally? That's an affront to heaven, to the dead, to nature, sheer absurdity to reason, whose main tenet is the death of fathers: if we didn't accept that we'd still be weeping today over the corpse of the first person who ever died. This is life. I urge you to bury this pointless sorrow and think of me as your father now."

Motioning with his hand, Claudius indicates the other people in the room.

"For let the world take note, you are next in line to the throne, and I offer precisely the same qualities of esteemed love to you which any fond father feels toward his son. As for going back to school in

Wittenberg, it is against our wishes. We would prefer it if you could remain here in the comfort and safety of the palace, our foremost courtier, dearest relative, our son."

"Don't let my prayers go to waste, Hamlet. I beg you to stay with us; don't go back to Wittenberg just yet."

"I shall do my best to obey *you*, madam," Hamlet assures her.

"A loving and devoted answer," Claudius smiles, with evident relief. "Consider yourself as regal as I in Denmark. Madam, come," he says, turning to the Queen. "This gracious and willing acceptance of Hamlet's brings me heartfelt joy; out of respect for which the great cannons will fire salutes with each jovial toast I propose today, the resounding thunder echoing in the sky throughout our rousing celebration. Come away," he orders, and the courtly entourage follows him out.

Hamlet remains on the steps in front of the throne. He looks down at his hands, forming one into a fist, which he raises to his lips and taps against his mouth, staring off into space for a moment before he lets the hand fall to the floor, studying it intently.

"If only this cold, solid flesh would melt, thaw and somehow vanish into thin air, like the dew... If only the Almighty hadn't commanded us against taking our own lives... O God! God, how worthless and tiresome the world's enterprises have become. Damn it... Damn it that my life is like an un-weeded garden, which has so completely gone to seed that things hideously overgrown have wrapped themselves around me. That it should all come to this! Only two months dead – no, not even two – so excellent a King, who, compared to this odious lecher was a god – so devoted to my mother that he wouldn't even let the wind blow too roughly on her face... But why am I forcing myself to remember this? Because she clings to Claudius as if she can't get enough of him! And all within a single month – I mustn't think of that – I won't – O Weakness...your name is Woman!" he erupts in disgust, his voice filling the empty room " – barely a month, the shoes as good as new she wore attending my father's coffin, sobbing uncontrollably – why, she – God, an animal with no ability to reason would have mourned longer – marrying my uncle, my father's brother – but as unlike my father as I am to Hercules. Married within a month, before the tears had even dried on her flushed cheeks – what degenerate haste! Leaping to get between the incestuous sheets as fast as she could! It *is* not, it *will* not come to good. But hold back, my heart, I must keep silent – "

Horatio, Marcellus and Barnardo having entered, Hamlet gets to his feet.

"Greetings your lordship!" Horatio calls as he approaches.

"How good to see you…" Hamlet murmurs vaguely, his mind still adrift in self-reflection. "You're looking well…Horatio, if I'm not mistaken."

"In the flesh. Your poor and humble servant, my lord."

"As I am yours, good friend," Hamlet says regaining his composure. A frown crosses his face. "But, why aren't you in Wittenberg? Hello, Marcellus."

"My good lord."

"It's wonderful to see you, Horatio – good day, sir," he adds, greeting Barnardo. "So tell me, what are you doing so far from Wittenberg?"

"Playing truant, my lord," Horatio winks.

"That I wouldn't believe had your worst enemy told me; it even hurts my ears to hear you say so yourself. You're not the truant type, Horatio. Come now, what brings you to Elsinore? Some instruction on the finer points of carousing?" he asks with a sarcastic grimace.

"No, my lord," Horatio replies. "I came to see your father's funeral."

"Please don't mock me, friend. It must have been to attend my mother's wedding."

"It was very soon after, my lord."

"Pure thriftiness, Horatio. Pure thriftiness. The hot food served at the funeral became the cold leftovers laid out for the wedding buffet." A pensive look on his face, he gazes at the throne. "I'd rather have watched my most detested enemy admitted to heaven than have witnessed that day, Horatio." He walks slowly over to the throne and sits down. "My father – I can see him now – "

"Where, my lord?" Horatio approaches the throne.

"In my mind's eye…"

"I saw him once," Horatio says. "He was a good King."

"He was a man, when all was said and done. I won't look upon one like him again."

"My lord, I think I saw him last night."

"Saw? Who?"

"Your father the King, my lord."

Shocked, Hamlet gets up from the throne and hastens over to Horatio. "My father the King?"

"I know it sounds amazing – "

"For God's sake, let me hear!"

"Two nights in a row while Marcellus and Barnardo were on watch, a ghostly presence resembling your father appeared in the dead of night. Clad from head to toe in his battle armor, he marched slowly and solemnly before them – once, twice, three times in all, no more than a few feet away – leaving them too stunned and terrified to speak. They came to me in confidence and described what had happened, so on the next night I joined them as they began their watch. Exactly as they had said, the apparition came again. I recognized the image of your father instantly, as much like him as my right hand is to my left."

Hamlet takes each of Horatio's hands in his own.

"Where was this?" he asks.

"High on the castle ramparts, my lord."

"Did you speak to him?"

"I did, my lord, but he, or it, wouldn't answer, although at one point it did lift its head and moved its mouth like it wanted to say something – only the rooster began to crow, scaring off the apparition. It vanished."

"This is incredibly strange, Horatio."

"On my life, it's true. We felt it was our duty to let you know."

"Of course, yet it disturbs me to hear this – are you on watch again tonight?" he asks Marcellus and Barnardo.

"We are, my lord."

"And you say it was wearing armor?" Hamlet asks Horatio.

"Full armor, my lord. From helmet down to the heels."

"You didn't see his face, then…"

"Actually, we did, my lord. He had his visor open."

"Did he frown?"

"He did, but more in sorrow than in anger."

"Was he pale or red-faced?"

"Ghostly pale."

"And did he stare at you?"

"All the time he was there," Horatio nods.

"I wish I'd been present," Hamlet says fervently.

"No doubt it would have astounded you as it did us."

"No doubt. Did it stay long?"

"Two, maybe three minutes."

"Longer than that," Marcellus offers, glancing at Barnardo.

"Not the time I saw it."

"His beard was gray, was it not?"

"Just the way it was when he was alive. Black with streaks of gray."

"I must watch for it tonight myself. Maybe it will appear again."

"I have a feeling it will."

"If it assumes the character of my father, I'll talk to it, though the fiends of hell might try to stop me. Have you kept this to yourselves…"

The three men nod.

"Good. Then perhaps you'll continue to do so, and whatever else happens tonight, not say a word to anyone? I'll make it worth your while. Farewell for now. I'll meet you on the upper platform between eleven and twelve."

"You can count on us, sir," Barnardo says.

"We'll do our duty, sir," Marcellus adds.

"Thank you, my friends." Hamlet shakes their hands, embraces Horatio. "Farewell until tonight."

When they have left, he turns back to the throne. "The ghost of my father – wearing his armor. All is not well; I know this means foul play. If only night would come! Till then stay calm, my soul; evil deeds will come to light, despite all efforts to keep them out of sight."

1.3

Dressed for traveling, Laertes meets Ophelia in the castle corridor coming out of her room.

"My personal things have been sent ahead, so I'll be on my way. If the winds are favorable and the ship makes good time, the trip should be a speedy one. Don't wait too long before writing to me."

They begin walking.

"What makes you think I would?" Ophelia asks her brother.

"As for Hamlet," Laertes says, ignoring her question, "and the apparently amorous advances he's made toward you, don't take them seriously. It's just his passing fancy, the impulsive whim of a moody young man – like the scent of a new spring flower which is strong and pleasing at first, but quickly fades. It's nothing more than that, sister."

"Perhaps not, but if – "

"Don't take him seriously," Laertes says firmly before she can explain. "Physical and spiritual growth don't always go hand in hand. He might appear to be one thing on the outside, however it's what goes on in here – " he taps his temple " – that really counts in shaping the true nature of who we are. Perhaps he loves you now, and his feelings are reasonably pure and uncorrupted. But you have to be wary because of the illustrious position he was born to inherit. The fact is, unlike common people, his life is not his own when it comes to making personal choices: the safety and well being of the country will eventually depend on his decisions, and so his wishes are subject to consideration by the state over which he will one day have supreme authority. Thus, if he says he loves you, bear in mind that ultimately he can only live up to whatever promises he makes to you if they are suitable for the future King of Denmark.

"You must understand how easily your reputation could be destroyed if you believe what he says in his poems, if you allow yourself to be seduced into surrendering your treasured chastity by mistaking persistence for genuine passion. Be careful, Ophelia, extremely careful. Don't let your feelings get the better of you. The most upstanding young woman can find herself the subject of vicious gossip just by confessing her secrets to the moon at night when she thinks no one else is around; virtue in itself is no guarantee you can escape malicious slander. Young flowers are vulnerable to things that aren't good for them, long before they're ready to blossom, in the same way young people are susceptible to the harmful effects of their intense emotions. Be cautious, Ophelia: don't turn a blind eye to your fears. Young and restless urges will only result in tears."

"I'll keep what you've said in mind in protecting my feelings. But please, dear brother, don't play the hypocrite and lecture me about the steep and difficult path to upright behavior, while you live a wild life of pleasure-seeking self-indulgence, ignoring your own advice to me."

"Don't give that a second thought," he says defensively. "Look, I have to get going – and here comes father. Well, I can say goodbye to both of you at the same time."

Polonius hurries importantly along the corridor toward his two children. Though he carries a cane, he seems to use it sporadically.

"Still here, Laertes? Get aboard, get aboard for goodness sake! A good wind is pushing at the sails – they're holding the boat for you." He places his hand on his son's bowed head and hastily utters a prayer. "There, my blessing goes with you – along with a few caveats you should store away for future use," he quickly adds. "For example, don't let people know exactly what's on your mind. Don't do anything without thinking it through completely. Be friendly to folk, but don't overdo it. The friends you have, those you know you can trust, cling to them with all your tenacity, making time for them as well as your new acquaintances, until you're sure of their reliability. Beware of quarreling, although if you end up in a tussle, be sure your opponent knows he's met his match. Listen to everyone's viewpoint, but give your own opinions sparingly. Similarly, consider the opinions of others but don't be quick to judge them. Wear clothes you can afford, always avoiding extremes of fashion. In other words, appear sophisticated without being gaudy, for clothes suggest what people should think of you. The most respected ranks of French society, for instance, are renowned for the impeccable quality of their attire. Don't borrow money and don't lend it out, either, for loans usually result in lost money and broken friendship. And borrowing hampers one's ability to be thrifty. Above everything else: be true to yourself and it will follow as night does day that you won't be false to anyone else. Goodbye, son, and let my blessing impress the value of this advice upon you."

Once again he has Laertes accept the touch of his hand and a muttered prayer.

"A humble farewell, my lord."

"Go, go!" Polonius says, shooing his son away. "Time is wasting – "

"Farewell, Ophelia," Laertes says, "and remember the things I said."

"I've locked them in my memory," she says obediently, "and only you have the key."

Bidding his sister a formal farewell, Laertes then departs.

"What is it that he said to you?" Polonius inquires, frowning curiously.

"Something concerning Lord Hamlet," Ophelia replies.

"A timely topic, indeed. I've heard that he's spending time alone with you, and that you have been very...open and generous with your feelings. If that's the case – and I'm told by people with your best interests at heart that it is – I must warn you, you don't know yourself as well as a daughter of mine should, or what this could end up doing to your reputation. What in fact is going on between the two of you? Let me have the truth."

"He has recently made numerous declarations of his affection for me."

"Affection? Bah! You talk like a little girl with no experience in playing such a dangerous game. Do you believe these 'declarations' as you call them?"

"I'm not sure what to think, my lord."

"Well, I will help you then. Think yourself naïve for assuming counterfeit items are the real thing. Be much more discreet with these 'declarations' or – not to let a good pun go to waste – you'll have people 'declaring' me a fool."

"My lord, he has professed his love for me in a very honorable fashion."

"Of course it's in fashion – fashionable nonsense."

"He swore in the name of heaven it wasn't."

"Of course he did. That's the trick for snaring a silly girl. Believe me, I know when the fires of passion begin to burn how eager lovers fan the flames with outrageous promises. But such blazes give off more light than heat, my girl – both of which have begun to go out by the time the promise is made – yet you can't take them for the flames of real love. From now on it would be best if you didn't appear in public quite so much. As well, don't agree to talk to him just because he wants you to. Remember Lord Hamlet, besides being young, enjoys greater freedom to do as he pleases than you. As for what he's promised, take it all with a grain of salt: his words are shrewd deceptions whose fervent ardor and breathless beseeching will turn out to be hollow and worthless in the end. There is no doubt about it. In fact, to prevent any further disgrace, I suggest you avoid Hamlet, period."

"Yes, my lord."

"Come along, then." Satisfied that Ophelia sees things his way, Polonius heads off, his daughter following obediently behind.

In the darkness atop Elsinore Castle, Hamlet, Horatio and Marcellus put out their torches before making their way slowly along the platform.

"It's freezing cold," Hamlet says, blowing on his hands to warm them.

"A chill in the air, that's for sure," Horatio concedes.

"What time is it?"

"Nearly midnight."

"No, it's past twelve now," Marcellus points out.

"Really? I didn't hear the bell sound," says Horatio, peering through the surrounding darkness. "It should almost be time for the ghost to – " His remaining words are drowned out by a loud flourish of trumpets and several booming rounds of cannon fire. "What does that mean, my lord?" he asks Hamlet.

"The King is up late drinking, toasting the health of one and all as he staggers around the dance floor quaffing Rhine wine, the guns and trumpets announcing he's polished off one more bottle."

"Is that a local custom?"

"More or less." Hamlet sits down on a ledge beside the castle wall. "Although to my mind, in spite of the fact I've grown up with it, the custom is one that's better ignored than observed. It makes us look like boors in the eyes of neighboring countries – they call us 'drunken pigs' and malign us with other demeaning phrases that disparage our good name abroad. Worst of all it takes away from our achievements as a nation and detracts from the worthy attributes that at one time earned us a respected reputation."

Horatio takes a seat beside his friend. Their breath rising in the frosty air, they ruminate quietly for a moment, listening for further cannon salvos, but none are heard.

"It happens to certain people…"

"What does?"

"Something in a person's nature is faulty," Hamlet explains, "something in their make-up from the time they were born – not what you can blame them for since we play no part in our own creation – and this trait comes to dominate the person, eventually breaking down the ability to reason, to maintain stability: a bad habit that goes unchecked and gradually turns them into a completely different person, all because of this particular defect Nature or Destiny put there. And despite the most impressive virtues, the most immense capacity for goodness, this particular flaw makes them go bad. Do you see?" Horatio considers the question in silence. "The smallest quantity of evil can transform the noblest soul into a consummate villain…"

Horatio suddenly shoots to his feet. "Look, my lord, there it is!"

Hamlet is up and moving toward a haunting human shape hovering close by. "Angels and heavenly hosts preserve us!" Hamlet cries. "Be you a blessed spirit or a fiend from hell, a celestial wind from above or a demonic tempest from below, be your presence hostile or friendly – you appear so strangely familiar I must speak to you. I'll call you Hamlet, King, father, royal Dane. Answer me, spirit. Don't keep me in stunned disbelief. Tell me why your consecrated body, already dead and buried, has unraveled its shroud – why the coffin in which we saw you solemnly laid has unclenched its great marble jaws and released you again into the world? What can it mean when a dead man dressed in his suit of armor comes wandering through the moonlight, like something from a nightmare, leaving us to imagine the horrors in store for us beyond the grave? Tell me why this is – why? What should we do?"

The ghost slowly lifts one of its arms and beckons Hamlet to come closer.

"It motions for you to follow it," Horatio remarks, "as if it wants to speak with you alone."

"How courteously it waves you to step away from us – but don't do it, my lord!"

"No, by no means, no!" Horatio agrees.

"It won't speak otherwise. I'll have to go where it wants me to."

"Don't my lord!"

"Why not? What is there to be afraid of? I don't place any value on my life, and as for my soul, how can one immortal thing do harm to another? It's urging me forward again. I'm going to follow it – "

"What if it lures you toward the water, my lord, the edge of the cliff where the castle juts out over the rocky shore hundreds of feet below, and then assumes some other ghastly form which could strip you of the power to reason so you descend into madness? Think of that. You know how the place itself plays desperate tricks on the minds of all who peer down at the sea where the waves crash against the jagged rocks."

"But it's waving to me – go ahead, I'll follow you," he tells the shimmering vision of his dead father.

"You mustn't, my lord," Marcellus cries, and takes him by the arms.

"Let me alone!" Hamlet cries, fighting to wrestle free.

Horatio lends Marcellus a helping hand. "Listen to us! You mustn't go!"

"My fate cries out and every artery in my body craves to know what it has to tell me. It's calling me. Let me go, gentlemen!" he protests, struggling to go with the ghost.

"I swear," he shouts, drawing his dagger, "I'll make a ghost of the man who tries to stop me. Stand back, I say!"

He turns to the ghost. "Go ahead, I'll follow you." And with that he starts along the platform and is swallowed up in the darkness.

"His imagination's running rampant," Horatio says frantically.

"We should follow him, Horatio. It's not right to stay back and do nothing."

"Let's go after him then," Horatio agrees and moves off across the platform with Marcellus. "Who knows what could happen if we don't."

"Something is rotten here in Denmark," Marcellus says ominously.

"Let's hope heaven will look after it– "

"Who knows, for now we'd best just follow him…"

As Horatio feared, the ghost has drawn Hamlet to the part of the platform where the castle overhangs a cliff high above the ocean.

"Where are you leading me?" he asks. "Speak to me here. I won't go any further."

"Mark my words," the ghost says in a grim voice.

"I will."

"The time has almost come when I must return to the sulfurous and tormenting flames."

"Alas, poor ghost."

"Pity me not, but listen carefully to what I have to say."

"Speak, I am eager to hear."

"So will you be for revenge when you have heard."

"What do you mean?"

"I am your father's spirit, doomed for a period of time to roam by night while during the day forced to do penance in hell until the dreadful sins committed in my life are burnt and purged away. If I wasn't forbidden to reveal what goes on in the place of my imprisonment, I could tell you a story whose simplest details would vex your soul, freeze your young blood, make your eyes leap out of their sockets, straightening your curls so every hair was standing on end like so many terrified porcupine's quills. But details of the eternal realm cannot be divulged to those who are still of flesh and blood.

Listen, listen, I call upon you to listen! If you ever loved your dear father – "

"Oh God!"

"Revenge his foul and monstrous murder."

"Murder!"

"Most heinous, most despicable, most depraved."

"Tell me how it occurred, so that with wings as swift as meditation or thoughts of love, I can seek revenge."

"You are up to the task, then. But of course you would be no better than a fat weed lazily rooted on the banks of Hell's River of Forgetfulness if a matter such as this couldn't stir you into action. Listen, Hamlet, and I will explain. People have been told that a serpent bit me while I was napping in the orchard – this is a false story that has been circulated to misinform the nation about the manner in which I died – but you most believe me, son, when I tell you the serpent whose sting killed your father now wears his crown."

"I thought as much – my uncle!"

"Yes, that incestuous, adulterous beast, with cunning shrewdness and treacherous scheming – so devious a mind, so wanton and sinister his powers of seduction that he succeeded in winning over my seemingly virtuous Queen with his vile lechery. O Hamlet, how dissipated she let herself become, after all she had been to me, whose love had never wavered from the vows made when we were married – stooping to the level of a worthless wretch whose inherent qualities were nothing compared with mine…"

The ghostly figure stays silent for several moments.

"Yet, just as genuine virtue remains steadfast even when lust comes courting disguised as divinity itself – so carnal desire, though it might be embodied in a radiant angel cannot stop craving satisfaction in the heavenly bed, even if that means preying on garbage. But wait, I think I detect the scent of morning air; I'll be brief. Resting in the orchard, as was my habit every afternoon, your uncle bided his time until I was fast asleep and then poured a vial of deadly hebona extract into my ear, the poison so fast-acting and lethal it spread instantly throughout my body like liquid silver, thickening my blood so that my infected skin broke out in leprosy-like scabs and pustules while I lay dying. This is how I was deprived of my life, my crown and my Queen, by my own brother – without opportunity either for the sacred last rites or the final absolution of my sins. Horrible, horrible," he moans in very real agony. "Most horrible…"

He fixes his eyes intently on Hamlet. "If it is in your nature, refuse to accept what has happened. Stand up and oppose the royal bed of Denmark being used as a place for wanton debauchery and outright incest. Just be sure that, by whatever means you go about this, you don't think or act harshly toward your mother. Let heaven be her judge, the thorns of her own conscience to prick and hurt her as they may. Farewell for now; the fireflies show me that morning is near, the rising sun causing their miniature lights to fade. Adieu, adieu, adieu. Remember me…"

And suddenly the ghost is gone.

"What in the world – what now? Shall I make a pact with the devil? I mustn't! Stand firm. Stand firm, my heart. And you, the sinews of my very being, don't let me down, carry me bravely forward. Remember you? Indeed, poor ghost, as long as memory has a place in this muddled head of mine. Remember you? Why, I'll erase every trivial, foolish thing hitherto recorded there, every proverb, impression, worry, observation or doubt I've ever known, so that your commandment alone shall be inscribed on every page in the book of my brain, purged entirely of all lesser matters. I swear to you! O loathsome woman…and you, O villain, villain. Smiling royal villain! My notebook – "

Hamlet rummages in a pouch attached to his belt and takes out a sheaf of writing papers, a small ink jar and a quill pen.

"In case something should happen to me I must get this down on paper." He readies himself, but his hand is shaking too much. "That someone can smile, and go on smiling, and yet be a villain – which at least I am sure is so in Denmark. Steady now," he says to himself and begins writing on his notepaper. "So, uncle…there you are. I must now be true to my word: 'Adieu, adieu, remember me.' I swear to you I will." He stops writing for a moment and gazes thoughtfully up at the sky, which is beginning to brighten in the east.

"My lord, my lord!" Horatio calls, a short distance away.

"Lord Hamlet!" Marcellus joins in.

"Heaven protect him."

"So be it," Hamlet says under his breath and quickly finishes writing before returning his materials to the pouch on his belt.

The first to spot Hamlet, Marcellus shouts, using a falconer's call. "Perch-ho, my lord!"

"Perch-ho, my boy. Over here, bird, over here."

By the time Horatio and Marcellus reach Hamlet he's pacing, brimming with excitement. "How are you my noble lord – what happened?" Hamlet looks away.

"I can't say. You'll tell everyone."

"No I won't, my lord. I swear," Horatio protests.

"I certainly won't, my lord," Marcellus declares.

"What would you say then, would you believe it possible – " Hamlet hesitates uncertainly " – would you promise to keep a secret?"

Horatio and Marcellus promptly swear they would.

"It's this. There's not only a villain living among us, but an evil-mongering demon."

"As if we need a ghost who has risen from the grave to tell us this, my lord," Horatio remarks with mild sarcasm.

The comment catches Hamlet off guard. "How right. How very right. And so without further fuss I think it's best we shake hands and go our separate ways, you as your work and dreams determine – for everyone has work and dreams, such as they are – while I, for my part, will go pray."

"These are confused and confusing words, my lord," Horatio observes with a frown.

"I am heartily sorry if they offend you," Hamlet replies brusquely, " – yes indeed, heartily…"

"Not offended, my lord – "

"Yes you are, Horatio, and very offended at that. But don't dismay. I assure you the apparition in question is a good and reputable ghost. As for your desire to find out what transpired between us, resist the urge to know. And indeed, good friends, since you are my friends – scholar," he glances at Horatio, "and soldier," he says with a look to Marcellus. "Let me make a request."

"What is it my lord? We will oblige in any way."

"Never make known what you have seen tonight."

"We won't, my lord," Horatio and Marcellus both reply.

"But swear that you won't," Hamlet says forcefully.

"I swear, my lord, I will not."

"I so swear, as well."

"Upon my sword," Hamlet says, drawing his weapon.

"We have sworn, my lord," Marcellus protests.

"Indeed, but upon my sword," Hamlet insists, gazing at something behind the two men. "Indeed…"

Swear!

"Ah ha, boy, what's that you say? Are you still lurking about?"

Horatio and Marcellus turn to look over their shoulders.

"Come. Do as he says. Swear," Hamlet orders.

"Propose the oath, my lord."

"That you'll never speak of what you have seen and heard tonight. Swear by my sword."

Swear!

Unnerved, Horatio and Marcellus do so immediately, just as Hamlet pushes between them and runs off along the platform.

"Hear and everywhere?" he calls out, almost merrily. "Then we'll meet you." A moment later he darts toward another part of the castle platform, looks around briefly, and then hurries back the way he came, Horatio and Marcellus doing their best to follow him. "Over here gentlemen, and place your hands on my sword."

Horatio and Marcellus join Hamlet and dutifully put their hands on the hilt of his sword.

"Now, swear by this sword you will never tell a soul what you have heard."

Swear by his sword!

Once again, they swear as instructed.

"Well old fox! You move fast! Aren't you the sly one!" Hamlet breaks away and dashes to yet another location on the castle roof. "Once more gentlemen!" he calls, "over here!"

"How much stranger can this get," Horatio grumbles in exasperation as he and Marcellus rendezvous with Hamlet once more.

"Stranger?" Hamlet asks. "Being a stranger, I thought you'd enjoy this. After all, there are more things in heaven and earth than you can account for with your philosophy, Horatio. Now come. As you did before."

He has them clutch the handle of his sword for the third time. "You will never, so help you, no matter how strangely or outrageously I behave – even if I go so far as to play the madman – swear that no matter what you see, you won't fold your arms, shake your heads and start saying things like 'We know what's going on', or 'We'd tell you if we could', or 'If we wished to', or 'There are those who might explain' – not the slightest insinuation or ambiguous comment that would indicate you know what I'm up to – swear this, for grace and mercy's sake, so help you."

Swear!

Marcellus and Horatio swear.

"Rest, rest, perturbed spirit!" Hamlet calls out across the platform. Sliding his sword back into its sheath, he turns to Horatio and Marcellus. "So, gentlemen, please accept my heartfelt gratitude; and whatever a poor man like I can do in return for your loving friendship, God willing, I shall. Let us go in together."

They begin walking, Hamlet following a few steps behind his friends.

"Keep fingers to your lips I implore you," he says, though not loud enough for them to hear.

Distracted, he slows down and gazes toward the horizon, where the sun is beginning to rise. "The time is out of joint," he murmurs to himself. "O cursed spite that I was ever born to set it right…" Horatio and Marcellus have stopped to wait for Hamlet to catch up.

When he does, Horatio throws an arm around his friend's shoulder. "Come, let's go inside…."

Reynaldo, a servant about the same age as Laertes, helps the elderly Polonius down the wide, white marble stairs until they reach an open foyer in the castle. In exchange for his cane, Polonius hands over a brown leather pouch and an envelope sealed with wax.

"Give him this money and these notes, Reynaldo."

"I will, my lord."

Polonius deposits the items in Reynaldo's hands, but continues to hold them.

"It would be especially helpful to make enquiries about his behavior before you visit him."

"I intended to do that, my lord."

"My word, a fine answer," Polonius laughs and releases the pouch and envelope into Reynaldo's care. "A very fine answer... So, here's what to do. Find out for me first what Danes are living in Paris, how they're fixed for money, family background, occupation, where they live, who they socialize with, spending habits, that sort of thing; and once you ascertain through this roundabout questioning process that they do in fact know my son, at that point, shift to a more specific strategy than your initial enquiries will allow. Suggest that you have a passing knowledge of this Laertes, as for example 'I happen to know his father, I've met some of his friends, I'm a casual acquaintance of his – do you see, Reynaldo?"

"Quite clearly, my lord," the servant replies patiently.

"'A casual acquaintance of his.' But, you could emphasize the 'casual' aspect, in that you say the person you happen to be acquainted with is a very wild, drink-addicted so and so' and at that point you improvise whatever outlandish stories you want – mind you, none so bad as to completely disparage him, be careful of that, just keep it to the usual reckless and randy antics a rambunctious young man would be known for among his friends."

"Such as gambling, my lord?"

"Yes, or drinking, sword-fighting, quarreling, flings with prostitutes – you can go as far as that."

"My lord that could disparage him, though."

"Not if you put the right slant on your words, for goodness sake. Just don't accuse him of anything too drastic, like an insatiable appetite for sex – that's not the kind of thing I had in mind; more that you would insinuate or merely imply certain things that are the pitfalls of having too much freedom, the stimulations and fantasies of an overactive imagination, a savage streak in his hot-blooded personality, things that attack his character in general."

"But my good lord – "

"Why should you do this?"

"Yes, my lord. I would like to know."

"Why, sir, here's my plan and I believe it's a positively effective one. By casting these minor aspersions against my son, which of course you accentuate and cleverly extenuate during the telling, that is to say by engaging a particular individual in conversation you inquire if he's seen evidence of the aforementioned vices in the aforementioned young man, of whose guilt you have actually been informed, why he will almost certainly respond in the following way: 'Good sir', or something like that, or 'friend', or 'gentleman', according to the phraseology or style of address fashionable in the society of that country."

"Very well, my lord," Reynaldo nods, not a little puzzled.

"And then, sir, he will do this – he will – what was I about to say? My goodness, I was about to say something. Where did I leave off?"

"'…Certainly respond in the following way.'"

"Certainly respond in the following way, ah yes, good. So he will respond 'I know the gentleman, I saw him yesterday' or 'just the other day' or at this time or that time, with so and so, 'and as you suggest there he was gambling', 'there he was passed out from drinking too much', 'there he was quarreling over a point in tennis', or possibly 'I did see him entering a house of ill repute' – that is to say a brothel, and so on and so forth. Then, you see, the lies you've used for bait will hook the fish of truth, which is the way we men of wisdom and discernment with shrewd tricks and subtle stratagems contrive to find out what we want to know in the most roundabout of all ways. Thus by taking my pointers and advice to heart, you can too, my son. You see what I mean of course?"

"Quite clearly," Reynaldo says with a look of befuddled consternation.

"God be with you then. Farewell."

"Thank you my lord."

"Be sure you keep a close eye on him, Reynaldo," Polonius adds.

"I shall my lord."

"Let him do whatever he has to do."

"Very well, my lord," Reynaldo says as he turns and hastens down the corridor, bowing to Ophelia whom he passes on the way.

Polonius notices the stricken look on her face.

"Good gracious, what's wrong Ophelia?"

"Oh my lord, my lord, I've been so terrified."

"By what, in the name of God?"

"As I was sewing in my room, Lord Hamlet appeared with his jacket undone, his shirt hanging open, his hair a complete mess, and torn, dirty stockings twisted around his ankles – pale and shaking all over as if he was having a seizure, with a tormented look on his face like he'd been sent straight from hell – thus he confronted me."

"Mad with love!" Polonius declares confidently.

"I don't really know, my lord, but I fear it could be."

"What did he say?"

"He seized my wrist and pulled me toward him very hard. Then he shoved me away and held me at arm's length, his other hand pressed against his brow while he studied my face as though he was preparing to sketch it in minute detail. He stayed this way for a long time until finally, jerking my arm and nodding his head up and down, he let out a plaintive sigh so poignant it seemed to shake him to the very core. Finished, he flung my arm away and with his head turned back over his shoulder all the while, he found his way to the door and left without taking his eyes off me for a second."

"Come with me," Polonius snaps, "we'll go and find the King. This is the very ecstasy of love, so overwhelming and all consuming that unlike the other passions it can force a person to behave in utterly desperate and destructive ways. I am sorry – unless, have you been hard on him recently?" Polonius inquiries as an afterthought.

"No, my good lord, I've only done what you instructed me to. I sent back his letters and refused to talk with him."

"Doubtless that is what has made him mad. I wish now I had paid closer attention to him. All along I was so worried that he was toying with your affections in a way that would put your reputation in danger – curse me for being overly suspicious in that regard, but by heaven it's only to be expected of those my age since the younger generation goes too far the other direction by not being vigilant enough. Come, let's go to the King. We must make this known, for the consequences of keeping it to ourselves until later are sure to be worse than raising such a touchy subject now. Come along."

After a flourish of trumpets signaling the arrival of the King, Claudius and Gertrude enter a state room in the castle, accompanied by an entourage of attendants and two courtiers, Rosencrantz and Guildenstern, friends of Hamlet from younger days.

"Welcome dear Rosencrantz and Guildenstern," Claudius begins. "Besides the fact we have not seen you in ages, our need for a favor prompted us to send for you so suddenly. You have no doubt heard something about Hamlet's recent…transformation as I call it, since he neither outwardly nor inwardly resembles his former self. What has precipitated this disturbing transition is quite beyond my comprehension. Thus I would appeal to the two of you, who have known him and been familiar with his personal behavior since childhood, to consider spending some time with us here at court so your presence can boost his spirits on the one hand, and on the other give you an opportunity to find out whether something we don't know about is affecting him so adversely – something which, if we knew what it was, we could try to remedy."

"Good gentlemen," Gertrude carries on, "he's talked about you so much I'm sure there aren't two men alive whose friendship he values more. If you would do us the honor and courtesy of extending your stay while we search for a solution to the problem we're facing, I assure you your efforts will receive the utmost in royal appreciation."

"Both your Majesties," Rosencrantz replies, "by the sovereign power you exercise, could as well put this matter in the form of a command as a request."

"But we both obey," Guildenstern is quick to add, " and place ourselves completely at your disposal to be commanded in whatever manner you see fit."

"Thanks Rosencrantz," Claudius says, offering him a grateful handshake, "and kind Guildenstern." The two men cover the King's mistake with polite smiles.

"Thanks Guildenstern," Gertrude says, correcting Claudius, "and kind Rosencrantz. I hope you can talk with my much-altered son as soon as possible. Go, some of you," she says, issuing an order to her entourage, "take these gentlemen to see Hamlet."

"Heaven make our presence and our practices enjoyable and rewarding for him."

"Amen to that," Gertrude sighs as the two are led out of the room, just before Polonius hurries in and approaches Claudius.

"I'm pleased to announce that the ambassadors from Norway have returned, my good lord."

"You are always the bearer of good news, Polonius."

"Am I, my lord?" Polonius replies with a modest shrug. "I assure you I value duty to my God and to my gracious King in equal measure, and I think – or else this brain of mine doesn't put two and two together as it used to – that I have uncovered the source of Hamlet's distress."

"Do tell me about that," Claudius says, visibly intrigued, "I'm most anxious to hear."

"Admit the ambassadors first," Polonius suggests. "My news can be the dessert to top off their sumptuous feast."

"Very well," Claudius agrees, though it is obvious from his tone of voice that he is impatient to hear what Polonius has to say. "Go greet them, then show them in if you would." While Polonius obeys, Claudius turns to the Queen. "He tells me, dear Gertrude, that he has got to the root of your son's problem."

"My guess is that his father's death and our hasty marriage are at the heart of it…"

"Well, we'll question him closely…"

Accompanied by the ambassadors Voltemand and Cornelius, Polonius returns to the state room and presents the two diplomats.

"Welcome, my good friends," Claudius says receiving them. "Tell me, Voltemand, what news from the King of Norway?"

"Not only does he heartily reciprocate your greetings and good wishes, but after our first audience with him he ordered his nephew to cease recruiting soldiers for an army which he assumed was preparing for a campaign against Poland, but which was actually intended for an attack on your Highness. Livid that his old age and declining health had been taken advantage of, he ordered his nephew Fortinbras to be arrested. In short order the young man confessed to deceiving his uncle, received Norway's stern rebuke and, finally, promised never to take up arms against your Majesty again. Pleased, Norway awarded him an annual stipend of 3,000 crowns provided he use the army he had raised against the Poles as originally intended. He also entreated us to give you this," Voltemand explains, handing over a document stamped in Norway's sealing wax, "seeking permission for his nephew's army to pass peacefully through Denmark, with all safety and good conduct protocols guaranteed."

"We do like the sound of this," Claudius responds, "and when there's more time we'll go over the particulars in detail. Meanwhile, we thank you for the diligent work you've done. Go and enjoy some rest and relaxation until the banquet tonight in your honor. Welcome home, gentlemen."

When Voltemand and Cornelius have departed, Polonius makes his way over to Claudius and Gertrude.

"Now that this business is over and done with," he begins self-importantly, "let me suggest, my gracious lord and lady, that to expound on the nature of true majesty, the components of duty, why day is day, night is night, and time is time, is merely to waste time, night and day . Therefore, since brevity is the very source and soul of clarity, and belaboring a point nothing more than ponderous showing off, I will by all means be brief. Your noble son is mad. I use the term 'mad' for, to define true madness merely becomes another form of madness. Be that as it may – "

"More matter with less art," Gertrude frowns impatiently. "Get to the point, Polonius."

"Madam, I swear I use no art at all," he protests. "That he is mad, it is true; that it is true, is a pity; and a pity it is that it is true. A foolish figure of speech, I must say," he offers with a self-satisfied smirk until he spots the annoyance in Gertrude's face. "But let that go," he carries on hastily, "for I will use no art in explaining. Let us accept that he is mad, then. What remains to be determined is the cause of this effect, or perhaps I should say the cause of this defect, for this defective effect comes from a cause. Therefore the explanation remains, and the remaining part of the explanation is this: Consider, if you will, the fact that I have a daughter – have as long as she is mine – who out of duty and obedience, it should be said, gave me this." He takes out a piece of paper tucked away in his cloak, and unfolds it. "Draw your own conclusions," he says, propping a pair of spectacles on his nose. "'To the celestial and my soul's idol,'" he reads, "'the most beautified Ophelia –' That's a trite phrase, an insipid one, 'beautified' is so bland. But you must hear – " He runs his eyes quickly down the page searching for passages worth quoting. "'These…'" he mutters. "'In her excellent white bosom; these – '"

"Hamlet sent this to her?" Gertrude wants to know.

"Patience madam, if you please. I will be as good as my word. Ah! 'Doubt you the stars are fire, doubt the sun in the sky above. Doubt truth itself to be a liar, But never, never doubt my love. O dear Ophelia, I am no good with words – I don't have the skill to describe the ache I feel. But that I love you best of all, O very best of all, please believe me. Adieu. Yours forever more, dear lady, while this body belongs to him known as Hamlet.' My ever-obedient daughter shared this with me and, more significantly, furnished me with details as to where, when and how he had been making his amorous overtures."

"How has she received them?" Claudius inquires.

"What do you take me for?"

"A loyal and upright man."

"And I sincerely hope to prove myself so. But what might you have thought when, having noticed love was beginning to heat up between the two of them – something I was able to detect even before my daughter told me about it – what might you or my dear Majesty your Queen have thought if I had chosen to take the part of go-between, or for sentimental reasons played the innocent bystander watching young love take its course – what, I wonder, would your Majesties have thought?"

Claudius and Gertrude are at a loss for words.

"Yet, have no fear, for I went right to work and spoke to my daughter: 'Lord Hamlet is a prince and quite out of your realm. There can be nothing between the two of you.' And then I instructed her to lock herself in her room if he stopped by to visit, turn away messengers that came knocking, accept no tokens of affection from him whatsoever. My lecture over, she heeded my advice, and he, rejected – to make a long story short – grew despondent, began starving himself, suffering insomnia, fatigue, dizzy spells, and slowly deteriorated into the raving madness which we are all mourning at the present time."

"Do you think this is it?" Claudius asks Gertrude.

"It could be; very possibly."

"Has there ever been a time," Polonius asks Claudius, "and I can't recall one myself, but has there been a time when I have positively stated 'This is so' and it proved otherwise?"

The King shakes his head. "Not that I can think of."

"Take this," Polonius touches his head, then makes a cutting motion across his throat, "from this, if it ever proved otherwise. Circumstances permitting, I will find out exactly where the truth lies, no matter how well hidden it may be."

"What should we do at this point?" Claudius wonders.

"You know how he likes to roam the corridors in this part of the castle for hours on end?"

"Indeed he does," Gertrude acknowledges.

"Next time he's about I'll send my daughter to talk to him. You and I," he meets Gertrude's eyes, "will station ourselves behind one of the wall tapestries and listen to what goes on. If he doesn't love her, and has not lost the ability to think rationally because he loves her so, then I'd be better with a horse and cart working on some farm than acting as a trusted state adviser."

"I suppose it's worth a try," Claudius decides, unaware that Hamlet has entered the state room, deeply engrossed in a book he is reading.

"There he is now, poor boy," says Gertrude, "reading to escape his sadness."

"Off you go the two of you," Polonius says brusquely. "Let me deal with him alone for now."

Claudius takes Gertrude gently by the arm. She hesitates, anxiously keeping her eyes on Hamlet while Polonius waves urgently for her to be gone. With a final glance at her son, she turns away and allows Claudius to lead her out, the royal entourage following briskly behind.

Polonius sidles up to Hamlet. "How are you, my lord?"

"Well, thank God," the Prince replies without looking up from his book.

"Do you know me, my lord?"

"Extremely well, yes." Hamlet looks Polonius straight in the eye. "You're a pimp."

"Not I, my lord!" says Polonius, taken aback.

"Then I wish you were as respectable as one."

"Respectable, my lord?"

"Yes, sir. Only one man in ten thousand is respectable these days."

"Very true, my lord," Polonius agrees, obsequiously.

"For if it's the sun that breeds maggots in a dead dog, and being one who preys on flesh himself – Do you have a daughter?"

"I have, my lord."

Hamlet glances about to make sure no one is listening, Polonius following his eyes around the empty room. "Don't let her go out in the sun," he whispers. "Conception is a blessing, but since your daughter may conceive – " He waves a warning finger. "Watch out, my friend..." He steps past Polonius and goes back to reading his book as he strolls through the stateroom.

"What does he mean by that?" Polonius mutters to himself, confused. "Still harping on my daughter, yet he didn't recognize me at first; and he called me a pimp. He's far gone, although it's true I went through something this bad when I first fell in love as a young man. I'll try again," he says decisively and walks up behind the Prince. "What is it you're reading, my lord?"

"Words, words, words."

"Of course. But what is the matter, my lord?"

"Between who?"

"I mean, your reading matter?"

Hamlet closes the book and regards it pensively for a moment. "Lies, sir. For the satirical rogue says here that old men have gray beards…" Polonius puts a hand to his wispy beard. "That their faces are wrinkled, their eyes discharge a thick, yellow fluid not unlike pine gum, and that they have an incredible lack of intelligence, plus their thighs are weak and their buttocks nothing but bone – all of which, sir, though I most powerfully and potently agree, still I find it a most unflattering portrait to have included in a book. As for you, sir, you will grow to be as old as I – if like a crab," and he suddenly advances on Polonius, who steps back in flustered retreat, "if you can walk backward like this." His feet tangling with his cane, Polonius begins to stumble but Hamlet catches his arm and keeps him upright. Then he promptly turns away, leaving Polonius to regain his composure.

"Though this is madness, there is some sort of method to it. – Perhaps you'd care to go outdoors, my lord."

"To visit my grave?"

"Indeed, that would be outdoors," Polonius concedes. "How apt some of his replies are – a cleverness that madness sometimes captures in ways that reason and sanity can't hope to. At any rate, I should probably leave him alone and work on arranging an encounter between him and my daughter. – My lord, I will take my leave of you."

"You cannot, sir, take from me anything I would more willingly part with – except my life, except my life, except my life."

"Farewell then, my lord."

"These tedious old fools," Hamlet sighs. He watches Polonius shuffle toward the stateroom door where Rosencrantz and Guildenstern have come in. They politely step aside to let the older man pass.

"If you're seeking the Lord Hamlet, he's over there," Polonius informs them, pointing toward the Prince with his cane.

"God bless you, sir," Rosencrantz offers in thanks.

"My honored lord!" Guildenstern calls as he heads across the room.

"My most dear lord!" Rosencrantz follows.

"My very good friends," Hamlet says in greeting and embraces each of them warmly. "How are you Guildenstern? Ah, Rosencrantz. Good fellows, how are the both of you?"

"Happy in that we're not excessively happy," Guildenstern allows. "Although we're not the peak of Fortune's cap."

"Not the soles of her shoes?"

"Nor that either, my lord."

"Then you're somewhere around her waist, or somewhat lower?" Hamlet teases.

"You could say we were her privates, yes," Guildenstern grins.

"Fortune's private parts. How true, she is quite the harlot. What's the news with you?"

"None, my lord, except the world's become too chaste for our liking," Rosencrantz pouts, putting his hands over his groin and shaking his head in mock sadness.

"Then doomsday must be near. But that's not what you came to talk about. Let me ask you, my friends: for what offence has Fortune sent you here to prison?"

"Prison, my lord?"

"Denmark's a prison – "

"Then the world is one too."

" – Its copious chambers, cells and dungeons making it one of the most notorious."

"We don't think so, my lord."

"Why then it can't be after all. For things are only good or bad if you think they are. To me it is a prison."

"Perhaps your ambition makes it one; perhaps Denmark's too

confining for a mind like yours."

"God, I could be enclosed in a nutshell and still consider myself a king of infinite space – if I didn't have such bad dreams."

"And what are dreams but ambitions, their substance merely the shadow of a dream."

"Dreams themselves are shadows…"

"Very true, and I maintain ambition is so insubstantial, so light and airy, it's nothing but a shadow's shadow."

"Then a beggar like me can become a somebody, and monarchs and boastful heroes can end up in the beggars' shadows. Shall we go and join the others at court?" Hamlet asks wearily. "I fear my reasoning powers are failing me."

"Your obedient and humble servants, my lord," the two friends respond in unison, making elaborate flourishes with their hands as they bow before Hamlet, who is unsettled by their suddenly formal manner.

"I don't look upon you as servants, by any means. In fact, right now I've had it up to here with those who profess to be at my 'service'. So be frank with me, between friends, what are you doing at Elsinore?"

"We came for no other reason than to visit you, my lord."

"My supply of gratitude being low these days, I have little to offer in the way of thanks, but I thank you anyway." He notices the two of them exchanging glances behind his back. "I'm sure greater thanks would cost me more than I can afford. Were you not sent for, or are you here of your own volition? Stopping by voluntarily? Come come. Be honest with me. Please, gentlemen. What do you say?"

"What should we say, my lord?"

"Anything except the main reason you've come: you were sent for, and there are guilty looks on both your faces which you don't have the craftiness to hide. I know the good King and Queen have sent for you to do their bidding."

"And what would that be, my lord?"

"*That* you would have to explain to me. But again, let me ask you honestly, as friends who have spent time together over the years, out of respect for 'the ties that bind', and all the fancy vows a better speaker than I could dream up, tell me the truth: were you sent for or not?"

"What should we tell him?" Guildenstern whispers to Rosencrantz under his breath.

"I have eyes, gentlemen," Hamlet reminds them. "For heaven's sake, don't play me for a fool."

"My lord," Guildenstern admits, "we *were* sent for."

Hamlet casts a benign smile at one and then the other. "I will tell you why, to save you the trouble of finding out for yourselves yet allow you to keep up a pretence of secrecy with the King and Queen. I have lately, although I don't really know why, lost the ability to be happy and renounced all that used to bring me pleasure. In fact I am so depressed that the beautiful earth itself seems like a sterile wasteland, this wonderful canopy of blue above – look there – this marvelous arch of sky hanging overhead, this majestic roof adorned with the sun's golden fire, why, to me it's nothing but foul, disease-ridden clouds of fog."

Rosencrantz and Guildenstern fidget uncomfortably when Hamlet trains his penetrating stare in their direction.

"What a piece of work is man, how noble in reason, how infinite in faculties, in form and movement how exact and admirable, in action how like an angel, in apprehension how like a god: the beauty of the world, the paragon of animals – and yet, to me, what is this quintessence of dust? Men don't delight me – nor women either, though by your smirks you seem to think so."

"My lord, I wasn't thinking that at all."

"Why did you laugh then when I said 'Men don't delight me'?"

"I was only thinking, my lord, what poor entertainment the players will be able to offer you. We passed them on our way here, eager for a chance to perform."

"He who plays the King is welcome – I'll be sure to pay his Majesty well; the bold Knight can wield his sword and shield as he woos his Lover, who won't sigh for nothing; the Moody Man can finish his part feeling good for a change, the Clown can bring laughter to the easily amused, the noble Lady speak her mind freely for once – even if she does have to break a few rules of poetic presentation. What company is it?"

"One of your favorites, the Chamberlain's Men from the city."

"How do they come to be on tour? I thought their regular theatre was more than suitable for making money."

"I believe they were banished from the city because of some controversy in which their patron was embroiled."

"But they're still held in high regard, still attracting a sizeable following?"

"Not any longer, I'm afraid."

"No? Why is that? Has their talent gone bad?"

"No, their work is still first-rate, but at present there's a brood of child actors, little nestlings who chirp and cry at the top of their comic voices in the private theatres, and the crowd can't get enough of them. They've become all the rage since they go out of their way to ridicule the public theatre companies, with the result that many accomplished actors are frightened their careers will be ruined by the satires of the upstart children."

"What? Children? Who supports them? How do they get paid? And what happens when their voices change? What if they stay on, join the adult stage companies as players themselves – as they no doubt will since there's no other way for them to make a living – aren't their writers doing them wrong by having them make fun of their future employers?"

"There's a great hue and cry from both sides about the situation, with audiences – who always enjoy a good fight – spurring the combatants on at every turn. For a while you couldn't raise money to mount a production unless the battle of the theatres was part of the play's plot."

"You can't be serious."

"It's become an all-out war."

"With the child actors getting the better of their elders?"

"Yes, my lord. Talk is that even the illustrious Globe is suffering."

Hamlet shakes his head and sighs. "It's not unusual, I suppose. My uncle is King of Denmark now, yet those who made fun of him when my father was King are shelling out forty, fifty, sometimes a hundred pieces of gold to buy a neck chain with a miniature picture of Claudius on it. I wonder if the philosophers will ever understand how human beings can be so fickle..."

The silence that follows is suddenly broken by a flourish of trumpets.

"That will be the Players," Guildenstern announces, he and Rosencrantz noticing the immediate change of expression on Hamlet's face.

In a better mood, he moves to shake their hands. "A polite and proper way of saying you are more than welcome at Elsinore. Let me take the opportunity to genuinely say so now, in case I appear to behave with more courtesy toward the players than I have toward both of you. You are most welcome here." At this point he brings them together and lowers his voice as if wanting to confide in them. "Though my uncle-father and aunt-mother are quite mistaken…"

"How so, my dear lord?"

"I am merely mad north-north-west. When the wind blows from the south, I can tell the difference between a hawk flying and a hawk in flight – "

His friends are trying to make sense of the remark when Polonius bustles into the stateroom again.

Standing between them, Hamlet puts an arm around each of their shoulders. "Listen, Guildenstern, and you too Rosencrantz – how convenient, a private audience for each ear – you see that great baby waddling toward us? He's still wearing diapers."

"Wearing them again, you mean. That's what happens during second childhood."

"I predict he's coming to tell me about the Players. Watch this." He turns his head and pretends to be deeply immersed in conversation with Rosencrantz. "You're right about that, sir, it was a Monday morning, I'm sure it was – "

"My lord, I have news for you," says Polonius.

"'My lord'," replies Hamlet, mimicking Polonius but not acknowledging his presence, "'I have news for you.' When Roscius was an actor in ancient Rome – "

"The actors have arrived, my lord."

"Buzz, buzz," Hamlet says obscurely, still looking away.

"Upon my word – " Polonius stammers awkwardly.

In slow motion, Hamlet turns and glares at Polonius. " – Then came each actor on his ass – "

"The best actors in the world," Polonius continues grandly, "whether for tragedy, comedy, history, pastoral, pastoral-comical, historical-pastoral, tragical-historical, tragical comical historical-pastoral, scenes in one location, poems in several, from Seneca to Plautus no tragedy too heavy, no comedy too light. For classical convention and less conventional present day forms, these are the best men around."

"Oh Jephthah, mighty judge of Israel, what a treasure you once had."

"What treasure was that, my lord?"

"Why, 'one fair daughter and no more, whom he did love so very much, yet later was to sacrifice, his only living daughter's life…'"

"Still going on about my daughter," Polonius remarks under his breath.

"Am I right old Jephthah?"

"If you insist on calling me Jephthah, my lord, I have a daughter and I love her very much."

"But that doesn't make sense."

"What doesn't my lord?"

"When I hear you say 'I have a daughter and I love her very much', for you know what happens in tragic Jephthah's story: 'It came to pass, as what most often is…' The first stanza of the old ballad will give you what you need to know, but look, here's my entertainment."

Decked out in costumes according to the characters they play – the King, the Knight, the Clown, the Moody Man, the Lady – the players approach and gather round Hamlet.

"You are welcome, masters. Welcome one and all. I'm glad to see you looking so well. – Welcome good friends. Why, look at this," he smiles at the King, "you've managed to grow a beard since I last saw you." Winking, he strokes his own bare chin "Have you come to poke fun at me? And what's this, my young miss," he asks the boy actor dressed like the Woman. "Look at your ladyship, a foot taller than when I last saw you. Let's hope your voice hasn't deepened accordingly. – Masters, you are all welcome. But let's not waste time, let's get things underway. Let's hear a speech – give us a sample of your work. Come, something passionate."

"What's your pleasure, my lord?" the leading Player inquires.

"I heard you rehearse a speech once, although it was never acted, or if it was, not more than a few times – for the play wasn't a crowd-pleaser, more like the taste of caviar for a general, which is to say not for public consumption. But from what I heard – and in the opinion of others whose judgment I respect – it was an excellent play, the scenes well structured, written with style and finesse. I remember someone said its quality came from the absence of cheap vulgarity and pretentious lines. I recall it was highly spoken of, a good, wholesome drama that was impressive in genuine rather than artificial ways. The speech I was most fond of – it was Aeneas's tale to Dido, particularly the part where he describes the slaughter of Priam, King of Troy. If you still know it from memory, begin at the line – let me see, let me see – *'Ruthless Pyrrhus, like the Hyrcanian tiger.'* No, that's not right. It begins with Pyrrhus – *'The ruthless Pyrrhus, he whose sable-crested arms, black as his purpose, so resembling the night when he lay hidden in the horse outside the walls of Troy, has smeared his dreadful black complexion bright with colored streaks more cruel – head to foot, grotesquely grimed with the blood of his enemies: fathers, mothers, daughters, sons, blood dried and baked with the heat from parchèd streets, the blazing sun lending its tyrannical and damnèd light to their lord's imminent murder: roasted in wrath and fire, covered with encrusted gore, his eyes aflame like hot red gems, the hellish Pyrrhus seeks the agèd Priam.'* You could carry on from there," Hamlet says to the leading Player.

"Well spoken, my lord," Polonius comments. "Fine emphasis and exactly the right tone."

"Before long," the leading Player begins in a stirring voice, *"Pyrrhus finds old Priam, King of Troy, striking at Greeks but every blow too short to hit its mark. His arm no longer strong enough to fight, his sword has lost its power to command. Unevenly matched, Pyrrhus falls on Priam, in rage strikes wide: the whiff and wind of his fell sword enough to blow old Priam to the ground. Then all of Troy, as if it felt the impact of the blow, collapsed in flames, its ancient walls and towers crashing hideously to earth, which sound took prisoner*

Pyrrhus's ear. And lo his sword – which fell to strike the white-haired head of Priam – seemed in the air to stop; so, like a painted tyrant, Pyrrhus stood, and like one who has lost the very will to move, did nothing...

"But as we often see before a storm a silence in the sky, the clouds standing still, the bold winds speechless, and the earth below as hush as death, soon the dreadful thunder split the air. So after Pyrrhus's pause, aroused vengeance set him back to work, and never did the Cyclops' giant hammers fall on Saturn's armor, forged to last forever, with less remorse than Pyrrhus's bloody sword then went at Priam. Out, out, you harlot Fortune! All you gods in general gathering take away her power, break all the spokes and axles from her wheels, and bowl the round rims down the hill of heaven to the depths of everlasting hell."

"This is quite long," Polonius says, interrupting.

"It's not something you trim like a barber does a beard," Hamlet explains, waving the leading Player to continue. "Please carry on. If it's not a farce or a bawdy tale he sometimes falls asleep. Go on, the part about Priam's wife."

"But who – ah woe! – had seen the mobbled queen – "

"'The mobbled queen'?" Hamlet frowns.

"That's good!" Polonius cheers, apparently understanding the word though Hamlet doesn't.

The Player carries on.

" – run barefoot up and down, threatening the flames so blinding were her tears, a rag upon the head where late a crown had stood, and, for a robe, about her lank and worn out loins, she clutched a blanket, caught up in the fury of her fear – she had seen all this, and shrieked in bitter rage that Fortune had betrayed her. But if the gods themselves did see her then, when she saw Pyrrhus make malicious sport by mincing with his sword her husband's limbs, the instant burst of clamor that she made, unless things mortal move them not at all, would have made moist the burning eyes of heaven, compassion in the gods."

"Look how his face has turned pale – " Polonius cries, pointing to the leading Player, " – he has tears in his eyes. Please, no more for now."

"Just as well," Hamlet agrees, helping the leading Player up from the floor where he lay crying. "I'll have you deliver the rest sometime soon. – If you wouldn't mind," he says to Polonius, "will you see that the players are well looked after? Remember they are the ones who record and report our history to posterity. When we're dead and gone it's better by far to have a bad epitaph on our gravestone than their disapproving verdict of our lives."

"My lord, I will treat them as they are deserving."

"Good gracious, man, do better than that. If you treat people as they deserve to be treated, most of them would be up for punishment. Give people dignity and respect whether they deserve it or not, and it reflects the merits of your own character. Go and look after them."

"Come, sirs," Polonius says and heads for the stateroom door.

"Follow him, friends. We'll have you do a play tomorrow." He turns to the leading Player. "Can I ask you a favor, old friend? Do you and your company perform *The Murder of Gonzago?*"

"Yes, my lord."

"That's what we'll have tomorrow night, then. And if you had to, could you insert a speech of perhaps twelve or sixteen lines, if I were to write it out for you beforehand?"

"Yes indeed, my lord."

"Very good." He points to Polonius shepherding the other Players. "Follow that lord, and make sure you don't make too much fun of him." He smiles and winks at the Player for the benefit of Rosencrantz and Guildenstern who are hovering nearby, uncertain as to what they should do.

"I'll see you tonight, good friends. Again, you are welcome here at Elsinore."

The two young men bow to the Prince and fall in behind the last of the players leaving the stateroom.

"Thank goodness," Hamlet remarks. "Now I am alone." He gazes quietly around the vast, empty room for several moments, steeped in the peace and quiet…"O what a weak and lowly drudge am I. Is it not unseemly that this player here, but in a made up story, a passion-filled dream, could evoke such feeling in his heart that the color drained from his face, tears poured from his eyes, distress showed in all his looks, with his voice cracking and his smallest gesture perfectly attuned to the part he was playing before us? And all for a simple performance. For Priam's wife! What's Priam's wife to him, or he to her that he should weep for her? What would he do had he the motive and the cue for passion that I have? He would flood the stage with tears, and hold the public's ear with his gruesome scenes, bring madness to the guilty and terrify the free, baffle the ignorant and leave the very faculties of eyes and ears amazed.

"Yet I, a dull and muddling fool, mope like a dreamer indifferent to the cause I've undertaken, and say nothing – not one word on behalf of a man whose kingdom was taken from him, whose precious life was destroyed. Am I a coward? Who calls me that? Cracks me across the head, plucks hairs from my chin and blows them in my face, twists my nose, pokes my eyes and then finishes with a blow that knocks the wind right out of me – who does this to me? God, I would likely stand there and take it: for I am nothing more than a coward, one who lacks the gumption to fight those who choose to treat me as such, or by now I would have thrown his body like rotting refuse to the vultures to feed on. Bloody, degenerate villain! Remorseless, treacherous, lecherous, monstrous villain! Why, what an ass am I, the loving son of a murdered father, prompted to take revenge by heaven and hell, yet like a whore I pour my heart out in angry threats, curse like a pot-scouring kitchen lackey. It's shameful… Disgusting…

"Think of something, brain. Think… I have heard that guilty people sitting at a play can find a scene so convincing it stirs their conscience and compels them to a confession of their crimes. Murder, though it has no tongue – but given such an opportunity – could speak, as if by some miracle it had one. I could have these players enact the murder of my father by my uncle, observe the expression on his face, be attentive to his every gesture. If he flinches, I'll know exactly what to do. The ghost I have seen may be the devil, and the devil is capable of assuming any shape he likes, and perhaps, taking advantage of my weakness and despair, he has put his potent and devious powers to work in order to deceive me into committing a damnable act. Therefore, I must find something that provides conclusive proof – the play's the thing wherein I'll catch the conscience of the King!"

The King, Queen and Polonius are meeting with Rosencrantz and Guildenstern in the castle rotunda, their voices echoing among the lofty stone arches. Ophelia arrives and hurries to stand with her father, the King acknowledging her bow before he resumes talking to Hamlet's friends.

"In other words, you can't understand from the things he said to you why he puts on this uncalled for confusion – disturbing others' peace of mind besides his own, with such wild and dangerous delusions?"

Rosencrantz shrugs. "He confesses that he feels himself 'on the verge', but of what, he refuses to say."

"Nor is he comfortable with us questioning him," Guildenstern explains, "but with a crafty shrewdness avoids telling us anything about what he's really feeling."

"How did he welcome you?" the Queen inquires.

"Like a true gentleman, although his politeness was clearly forced and stiffly formal."

"He barely asked questions of us, but was more than happy to answer ours, mind you in superficial or joking ways."

"Did you invite him to join you in some amusement?"

"It so happened, madam," Rosencrantz says, "that on the way here we met a troupe of traveling actors. We informed him of this and he was very interested to hear about the encounter. They are somewhere in the castle now, and I'm led to believe he has asked them to give a performance tonight."

"Quite true," Polonius pipes up, stepping forward. "And he asked me to be sure and invite your Majesties to come and see the play."

"By all means," the King declares. "It's certainly good news to hear something has put him in a better mood. Make sure you encourage him to enjoy whatever these players have to offer."

"We shall, my lord."

Rosencrantz and Guildenstern bow and head off, the King turning to the Queen.

"Sweet Gertrude, leave us too, for we have secretly arranged to have Hamlet pass this way so he can accidentally meet Ophelia. Her father and I, standing nearby but unseen, will judge from his behavior during the encounter whether or not it's love that's troubling him."

"Of course," says the Queen, stopping as she passes Polonius and his daughter. "And in that regard, Ophelia, I would like to think it is the bounty of your beauty that is causing Hamlet's distress; at the same time I hope your charms will make him his old self again, for both your sakes."

"I hope so too, madam."

Bowing as the Queen departs, Polonius places his hands on Ophelia's shoulders and guides her across the rotunda to a spot he has chosen.

"Ophelia, you will come walking along here, while we – your Majesty, if you please – will station ourselves over there behind the stairs so we can hear everything. Pretend you're reading this book to account for the fact you're alone. We often resort to this," he adds in his preachy tone, " and in fact it's been repeatedly proved that by putting on a good enough face, we can convince the devil to believe we're sincere."

In position under the stairs, the King ponders Polonius's comment uneasily.

"That is very true. How those words prick my conscience. The harlot's face, covered in attractive make-up, is no worse in the way it's used, than are the fraudulent words with which I have disguised my misdeeds. What a burden I've chosen to bear..."

"I hear him coming, my lord!" Polonius warns the King. "We must move out of sight!" He hurries to join the King, motioning Ophelia to begin reading.

In a moment Hamlet appears above, a somber look on his face as he slowly approaches a landing that overlooks the rotunda.

"To be, or not to be, that is the question: is it nobler in our minds to endure the strife and hardship fate inflicts, capriciously at best, or should we take a stand and, by resisting, fight until the troubles that we face are put to rest? To die is but to sleep, when all is said and done; and by that sleep, we bring an end to heartache and the suffering that plagues us all our lives. This is what, throughout our days, we long for: to die, to sleep; to sleep, perhaps to dream – yet that is what we truly fear: for in the sleep of death, the world of human turmoil far behind, the dreams we'd have – this is why we wonder so, why living lengthy lives is hard, for dreams, in death, go on forever…and from them no one wakes."

Hamlet starts down the stairs toward the rotunda.

"Why else would we bear the slights and slanders of this life, the oppressor's cruelty, the proud man's contempt, the pangs of unreciprocated love, the putting-off of justice, the disdain of those in high office, the scorn of idle boors, when freedom from all of this could be ours with the brief work of a knife? Who would continue to bear unwieldy burdens, laboring and toiling miserably on in life, if the dread of what happens after death – in the undiscovered country from whose domain no traveler returns – were not so horrifying as to make us prefer the troubles that we know, to those we don't? This is how conscience makes cowards of us all; the inborn desire to help ourselves succumbs to doubt and weakness, and plans for great and worthy deeds are set aside and never put in action."

Coming down the last few stairs, Hamlet enters the rotunda.

"Well," he murmurs to himself, "what's this? The fair Ophelia. Nymph, remember to include forgiveness of my sins in all your prayers."

"Certainly, my lord. But how have you been these past few days?"

"Well, I humbly thank you."

"My lord, I have some things you sent me which I have been waiting to return." She holds out a small silver box and the bundle of letters her father showed the King and Queen. "Would you be good enough to take them?"

Hamlet regards the items with a dull stare. "You must be mistaken. I never gave you anything."

"My worthy lord, you know very well you did. And with them words of fondness which made these things more meaningful. This affection now lost, I would like you to take them back, for rich gifts become poor ones when the giver stops caring. There, my lord."

She sets the silver box and the letters down on a stone pedestal close by.

"Ha-ha!" Hamlet shouts bitterly, glaring at Ophelia. "Are you virtuous?" he asks.

"My lord?"

"Are you beautiful?"

"What are you saying my lordship?"

"That if you are virtuous and beautiful, it's very dangerous to let the one converse with the other."

"Could beauty converse with something better than virtue, my lord?"

"It could, for the power of beauty can more easily transform virtue into its promiscuous opposite, than the strength of virtue can shape beauty into its own likeness. This was always assumed to be a paradox, but recent events here in Denmark have shown it to be absolutely true. I did love you at one time."

"Indeed, my lord, you led me to believe so."

"You shouldn't have believed me; for all the virtue in this world can't hide what's bad in us – it always finds a way to show through. Hence this fact: I never loved you."

"Then I was deceived – "

"Get to a nunnery!" he explodes cruelly. "Perhaps convent life – unless, do you want to breed sinners rather than pray for them? I myself am somewhat moral, though I could be accused of such acts it would be better if my mother had never brought me into this world to contemplate: I am far too proud, vengeful, and ambitious for my own good, with more harmful deeds in mind than I have thoughts to explain them, imagination to describe them, or time in which to commit them. What should men like me do while we slither here between heaven and earth? We are vicious scoundrels; don't believe a thing we say. Now, as I told you, get to the convent." He glances quickly around the rotunda. "By the way, where's your father?"

"At home, my lord," Ophelia replies, nervously confused.

"Make sure the doors are kept closed then," Hamlet says, lowering his voice in mock concern, "so he can play the fool nowhere but in his own house. Farewell." He then turns abruptly and walks away.

"Dear heaven, please help him…"

Hearing this, Hamlet suddenly runs back and takes her hands in his. "If you do marry," he says, exuding false sincerity, "let me leave you with this warning: whether you're pure as ice or clean as the driven snow, you won't escape slander. Now, off to your convent." He lets go of her hands. "Farewell. Or," he says the next moment, taking her hands again, "if you must marry, marry a fool; for wise men know what monsters you turn them into." He gives a winking smile, throws down her hands, and turns to leave. "The convent!" he shouts over his shoulder. "Quickly! Now farewell…"

"Heaven, restore him to his right mind!"

Passing the stone pedestal, Hamlet picks up his letters and the silver box. He gazes at them but again turns back to Ophelia.

"I know the way you color up for us," he hollers in disdain. "– the way your God-given faces, though perfectly good, are smeared with make-up to create new ones. The way you flirt and tease, pout and flaunt, using God's own creatures' nicknames to entice us – 'Why not some ass? Some cock? Some puss?' Pretending you can't help yourselves, the words just seem to slip out, you say. Come, come – I'm sick of it. What do you think has driven me mad?" He pauses. "I say we'll have no more marriage. Those married already – all but one – shall thrive; the rest shall not. To a convent. Begone!"

With this, Hamlet slips away down the adjacent corridor.

"O, what a perfect mind has been destroyed! The courtier's eye, the scholar's tongue, the soldier's sword. The country's hope and future, the epitome of good taste, the model of refinement, the one looked up to by so many, now utterly cast down. And I distraught and hurt as any woman can be – who took the sweetness of his promised love to heart – must see firsthand how his excellent powers of reason jangle, harsh as church bells out of tune, his handsome, young features ruined by raving madness. That my own sadness should be so – to have seen what I have seen and now see what I see…"

Tears welling up in her eyes, Ophelia holds the book over her face as the King storms from his hiding place, Polonius right behind.

"Love!" the King explodes in exasperation, "amorous affections have nothing to do with this, and what he said, though somewhat muddled, was not at all the garbling of a madman. There's a deeper, darker mischief he has in mind, and my suspicions lead me to believe that his troubled behavior poses an imminent threat to the kingdom; to prevent which, I have made my final decision: I'm sending him to England immediately, to retrieve an outstanding debt we are owed. Hopefully the sea voyage and the different surroundings will dispel whatever it is that's distressing him, which, though his brain's working quite the way it should, is forcing him to be most unlike his usual self. What do you think?" he inquires of Polonius.

"It seems to me the right thing to do. But I still believe the origin and beginning of his despondence has sprung from rejected love. So then, Ophelia – no need to tell us what Lord Hamlet said; we heard it all." A frown of displeasure when he sees her crying, Polonius plucks the book from her hands and steps forward to address the King. "My lord, if it's all right with you, after the play tonight have the Queen ask to see him alone, to talk about his…malaise, let her be open with him, and I'll be so positioned, with your permission, of course, as to hear every word they say. If she still finds him unwilling to give her satisfactory answers, then by all means send him off to England. Or at the very least have him confined in such a manner as your Majesty thinks best."

"Let it be so. Madness in great ones must not unwatched go…."

Early that evening, in the great hall where command performances take place, final preparations are underway for *The Murder of Gonzago*, the play Hamlet has requested from the players. Servants are working quickly to set up chairs in front of the stage area where the Prince himself, surrounded by men and boys attaching the draperies that will serve as curtains, has taken the chief Player and two others aside to make a point about the upcoming performance.

"If you can manage it, I would prefer the speeches go something like this: *Thoughts black, hands ready, poison mixed, timing right; this moment favorable, not a witness in sight* – Speak fluidly, smoothly, giving the phrases an emphasis of feeling, not merely bellowing and rhyming them off, like many actors do, as if they were competing with the town crier when he barks out the latest news. Control your hand gestures too, so they're more like this – " he says, showing the actors a graceful movement of his arms to illustrate what he means, " – so they complement the words you're using at the time. Even though you're supposed to be swept away with overwhelming emotion, you must keep a sense of moderation in order to make your performance believable and your feelings seem genuine. It makes me mad when I see one of these boisterous, blustering types tearing passion to pieces as though it's a shirt he's ripping up into smaller and smaller rags, purely for the benefit of the crowd in the back rows who, for the most part, don't respond to the meaning of the words as much as the various sounds and outlandish gestures accompanying them. Indeed, if I had my way, players guilty of overdoing things – acting more like King Herod than Herod himself would have acted – would be soundly punished. Please make an effort to avoid that."

"We will, my lord," the chief Player nods.

"At the same time, however, don't be timid. Use your own discretion. Match what you're saying with actions that will further the understanding of the words, and create your actions from an understanding of the character you're playing, keeping in mind a straightforward simplicity at all times. For anything artificial and exaggerated detracts from the purpose at hand, which is to hold a mirror up to human nature, showing virtue in its own right, foolishness and scorn as they naturally occur, society for what it is in all respects. Overplaying or underplaying, while either can elicit barrels of laughter from the uninitiated, only disappoints the seasoned playgoer, whose criticism, as I'm sure you would agree, takes priority over all other considerations in the theatre. I mention this because there are actors whose performances I have seen – and heard others praise highly –

who in my admittedly blasphemous opinion were incapable of portraying the speech or behavior of real people at all, strutting and hollering so ineptly their depiction of human beings was just abominable."

"I hope we have abolished that kind of thing, my lord."

"Abolish it completely, I say. And be sure your clown characters stick to the text as written – for there are those who like to ad lib and sometimes step out of character altogether in order to get a response from the audience, while neglecting, in the meantime, some of the major themes the play is attempting to deal with. That I find disgraceful, because it shows a pitiful desperation in the actor who – " He breaks off when he spots Polonius, Rosencrantz and Guildenstern entering the hall. " – honestly thinks he will get ahead that way. Now, go and get ready. How now, my lord Polonius. Will the King come and watch this masterpiece?"

"And the Queen too, as soon as it's time."

"Go and tell the Players to make haste, then."

Polonius nods and leaves to convey the message.

"Why don't the two of you go as well?" Hamlet suggests to his friends. "In case he needs you."

"Yes, my lord," says Rosencrantz and moves to follow Polonius, coming back for Guildenstern, who is intrigued by the lifelike garden setting the players have created. As the two of them leave with Polonius, Horatio comes out from behind a curtain and for a moment has the stage garden to himself.

"Horatio!" Hamlet calls to him a moment later.

"Here, my very friend," he replies, making a dramatic but mock gesture of obedience. "At your service, my lord."

Glad to see his friend, Hamlet moves toward the stage and watches while Horatio appreciates the set the Players have prepared.

"Do you know, you're the most honest person I've ever met," Hamlet says.

"My lord – " Horatio protests quietly.

"It's true. I'm not just flattering you. What would be the point of that? Why flatter someone with no money, who feeds and clothes himself through the generosity of those who admire the qualities of his character?" He pauses. "No, let the sugary compliments go to pompous fools and their fawning followers with well oiled hinges for knees, who believe their advancement will come with enough bowing and scraping. Are you listening to me?"

Horatio nods, Hamlet moving to stand beside him on the stage.

"Since my soul was able to decide for itself, and could distinguish good men from among the rest, it has held you close, Horatio. You are the same whether you're suffering a great deal or none at all, one who takes Fortune's blows and blessings in equal measure. How rare are those whose passions and good judgment are mingled so well that Fortune can't play them like stops on a flute any way she chooses. Give me a man who is not passion's slave and I will house him in the chamber of my heart, in my heart of hearts – which is what I have done with you."

Moved by the depth of Hamlet's feeling, Horatio looks away.

"I see I've said too much," Hamlet murmurs to himself. " – Well, there is a play being performed shortly in front of the King. The events in one scene correspond exactly to the circumstances of my father's death, as I explained them to you. If I might ask a favor, I would appreciate you keeping a sharp eye on my uncle during that particular scene. If the guilt he's concealing doesn't reveal itself when a certain speech is delivered, then it is clearly a sinister ghost we have seen, and the visions in my imagination are dark and depraved. Watch him closely, for my eyes will be riveted on him too. When the play is done, we will compare what each of us saw."

"Certainly, my lord. I will make sure nothing he does escapes my notice."

Trumpets and kettledrums sound a regal flourish from the back of the great hall.

"They are coming to see the play," Hamlet says. He and Horatio quickly leave the stage. "I must go back to playing my other self," he says matter-of-factly. "Find yourself a place to sit…"

Escorted by guards carrying torches, the King and Queen, Polonius and Ophelia, and Rosencrantz and Guildenstern take their seats, several dozen attendant lords and ladies assembled around them. When all are placed, the guards set their torches in holders to provide light for the stage.

"How does our cousin Hamlet?" the King inquires.

"Excellent, indeed, like a dish fit for a chameleon – I eat the air's different colors and find myself a changed man. But you can't feed chickens that way."

"I can make nothing of that answer, Hamlet. These words make no sense to me."

"Nor to me either." He turns from the King to Polonius. "My lord, you acted during your university days, you say?"

"That I did, my lord, and was acknowledged to have been a good actor."

"And what did you enact?"

"I did Julius Caesar. I was killed in the Capitol. Brutus killed me."

"What a brute to have killed such a capital fellow," Hamlet teases. "Are the players ready?"

"They await the signal to begin."

Hamlet gives Polonius a nod and he motions for the players to get underway. Taking note of where Horatio is positioned, Hamlet moves toward the King and Queen.

"Come sit with me, my dear Hamlet," Gertrude says.

"No, good mother," he responds, moving over to where Ophelia is sitting. "Here's metal that's more magnetic." He fastens his eyes on Ophelia.

"Ah-hah!" Polonius says to the King under his breath. "Did you hear that?"

Lying down at her feet, Hamlet gazes up at Ophelia. "Should I lie in your lap, Lady?"

Ophelia folds her hands and sets them discreetly on her lap.

"No, my lord."

"I mean, shall I put my head in your lap."

"I know, my lord."

"Ah! You thought I meant your country part – "

"I thought nothing, my lord," Ophelia protests, somewhat embarrassed.

"That's an odd thing to place between a woman's legs."

"What is, my lord?"

"Nothing."

"You are merry, my lord."

"Who, I?"

"Yes, my lord."

"Indeed, your very own jesting fool. What else can a man do but be merry? Just look at how cheerful my mother is, and my father barely two hours dead."

"No, my lord, it is two months now."

"That long? Let the devil wear his funeral black garb. I'm putting on my best sable coat. My word, dead two whole months and not forgotten yet! Then there's still hope the memory of a great man may outlive him by as much as half a year. Though by God he better put up some churches or there'll be nothing to remember him by. He'll be forgotten like the old-time buffoon, whose epitaph is all that's left him now: 'Some boohoo, while others swoon, for the long-ago, lost buffoon.'"

The trumpets sound and the play begins with a pantomime.

A Player King and Player Queen come silently on stage and embrace each other. She kneels before him and makes a show of her unworthiness. He takes her hands and has her stand up, then kisses her lovingly on the neck. He lies down on a bed of flowers. The Queen, seeing him asleep, leaves him and goes off stage.

Soon another man appears, Lucianus, who removes the King's crown, kisses it, pours poison from a vial into the sleeping King's ears, and then leaves the stage. The Queen returns, finds the King dead, and is instantly distraught. Lucianus the poisoner comes back with three or four other men. They try to console the Queen, who has the dead body carried away. The poisoner Lucianus woos the Queen with gifts. She resists him at first, but gradually accepts his love. The characters swiftly leave the stage.

"What's the point of this, my lord?" Ophelia wonders.

"Why, dastardly deeds. Mischief is the point."

"Is it meant to foretell how the story will unfold?"

The Player designated to speak the Prologue comes on stage.

"We'll find out from this fellow," Hamlet says in answer to Ophelia's question. "Players can't keep secrets: they tell all."

"Will he tell us what the mime show meant?"

"That he will, or any other show you care to give him," Hamlet says suggestively. "No need to be ashamed of showing; he certainly won't be ashamed of looking..."

"You are the one who should be ashamed. I think I will concentrate on the play."

The Prologue Player begins:

> *"For us and for our tragedy here*
> *We ask your kind indulgence,*
> *And also beg of you your utmost patience."*

He bows quickly and runs off stage.

"*This* is a prologue?" Hamlet objects.

"It was quite brief, my lord," Ophelia agrees.

"As a woman's love," Hamlet says.

The Player King and Queen from the pantomime reappear on stage and take their places. The Player King begins:

> *"Thirty times the chariot sun has overhead gone round*
> *The vast blue sea and planet earth's revolving ground;*
> *And thirty dozen moons with light's reflected sheen*
> *About the world have times twelve thirties been*
> *Since love joined us together, hearts and hands,*
> *United by our vows and wedding bands."*

The Player Queen replies:

> *"So many journeys may the moon and sun*
> *Make us count again before our love be done.*
> *But woe is me, you are so sad of late,*
> *So far from cheer and from your former state*
> *That now I worry, but don't be angry that I do,*
> *For women's fear and love are one, not two.*
> *How strong my love is, I think you know,*
> *And as my love has strength my fear does also.*
> *When love is great, the smallest doubt can turn to fear;*
> *This small fear growing great, great love as well grows there."*

The Player King responds:

"Sadly, I must leave you, love, and shortly too:
My faculties grow weak, my life's days, nearly through;
You will go on in this world I leave behind,
Admired and beloved, a new and loving husband to – "

The Player Queen protests:

"Don't let me hear the rest,
Another love would be treason in my breast.
If I take a second husband let me be cursed:
No one marries twice unless she's killed the first."

"A bitter shame," Hamlet says to himself, glancing at his mother as the Player Queen continues:

"A second marriage is but for social gain,
Not love the heart can long sustain.
A second time I kill my husband dead,
The night my second husband takes me to his bed."

The Player King answers:

"I do believe you feel the words you speak,
But firm determination oft turns weak.
Best intentions live through memory's mercy:
Strong at first, with time they fade so quickly.
As unripe fruit still on the tree,
No shaking can remove till it is ready.
Most necessary of all, you must forget
What you've resolved, not pay a self-owed debt.
Things in the heat of passion we propose,
The passion over, their point we gradually lose.
The extremes of either grief or joy
By their own nature themselves destroy.
Where in great joy we revel, in great grief we lament;
Grief can rejoice, joy can lament,
Between them there's little that's different.
This world is not for all, nor is it strange
That even our loves can with our fortunes change –

For it's still a question left to prove
Whether love makes our fate, or fate our love.
When a great man falls, watch how his following flies;
A poor man who does well, makes friends of former enemies.
And true to that extent, love on fortune usually depends:
For one who has no needs shall never lack for friends,
Yet when in need we make our friends too fast
We always find the friendship does not last.
Thus properly to end what I've begun,
Our wills and fates in two directions run,
Plans devised are often overthrown:
The thoughts are ours, the outcome not our own.
Though now you will no second husband wed,
Your thoughts will change as soon as I am dead."

Again the Player Queen protests:

"May earth refuse to give me food or heaven any light,
Lock up my rest and pleasure day and night,
Turn my hope and joy to desperation,
My comfort no more than a prison hermit's ration,
Let grief that robs the face of joy,
Take all that should end well and it destroy,
Both now and ever after send me lasting strife,
If once I am a widow, I again become a wife."

"If she should break it now – " Hamlet smirks.
The Player King responds to his wife:

"A heartfelt vow, my sweet, now leave me be;
I need some sleep, my eyes are heavy, my spirit growing
weary."

The Queen:
"Rest, my love, and soothe your head and heart,
And never let ill fortune drive the two of us apart."

As her husband lies down and closes his eyes, the Player Queen leaves the stage.

"Madam, how do you like the play?" Hamlet asks his mother.

"I think the lady protests too much."

"But don't worry, she keeps her word."

"Do you know the outcome of the story? Is there anything offensive set to happen?"

"Not at all, they merely jest – poison in jest. There's nothing offensive in the least."

"What's the play called?" the King inquires.

"*The Mousetrap* – such a clever play on words. It depicts a murder that occurred in Vienna – Gonzago is the Duke's name, his wife Baptista – you'll see in a moment. It's a poignant little work, but what of that? Your Majesty and those of us with a clear conscience have nothing to worry about. The guilty may flinch; we have no reason to."

At this point the man named Lucianus comes on stage and creeps stealthily up behind the sleeping Player King.

"This is Lucianus, the King's nephew," Hamlet announces for all in the royal party to hear.

"You're as good as a narrator, my lord," Ophelia remarks.

"I could narrate the story of you and your love if I knew who was pulling the strings," Hamlet gibes.

"You are full of cutting comments, my lord."

"It would cost you some labor to take off my edge."

"For better or for worse."

"Vow of the Miss-taken husband. – Begin, murderer," Hamlet calls to Lucianus. "Enough frowning faces. Just get on with it. The angry raven caws to see revenge…"

Standing over the sleeping Player King, Lucianus begins:

> *Thoughts black, hands ready, poison mixed, timing right;*
> *At last the favorable moment, not a witness in sight.*
> *This poison mixture, from deadly weeds collected,*
> *By witches cursed three times and thrice infected,*
> *Your natural power and fatal intensity*
> *This sleeping man's life destroy immediately."*

He carefully removes the top from his vial and pours the poison potion in the Player King's ears.

"He kills him in the palace garden that will soon be his," Hamlet points out. "The King's name is Gonzago. The play is based on a real story, written in choice Italian. You'll see in a moment how the murderer wins the love of Gonzago's wife."

"The King is getting up from his chair," Ophelia whispers to Hamlet.

"What, frightened by the Prologue?"

"What's wrong, my lord?" the Queen asks, quickly rising from her seat with a look of concern on her face.

"Call off the play," Polonius orders getting to his feet.

"Give me some light. Make way," the King says, perturbed.

"Lights, lights, lights!" Polonius cries as the King storms past him and out of the room. Waving the guards to grab their torches and stay with the King, Polonius takes charge of the commotion and ushers the Queen and the royal entourage out of the hall.

When Horatio and Hamlet are the only ones left, the Prince sits down in the King's chair, heady with the excitement he's provoked.

"*'Why, let the wounded deer go weep,'*" he says, reciting from a poem. "*'The buck, unhurt, shall play; for some must watch while others sleep, this is the world's way.'*" Wouldn't this, a feather-plumed hat and some stylish French shoes earn me a partnership in a company of players if I fell on hard times?" he asks Horatio.

"Half a share, perhaps."

"*'A whole one, I. For you must know, my loyal friend so dear, this realm has been abandoned, it's now become the laughing stock, the Kingly man who now reigns here, a right and royal pea...hen?'*"

"You could have made the rhyme," Horation smiles.

Hamlet shrugs indifferently. "O good Horatio, I'll bet a thousand pounds on the ghost now. Did you see?"

"Very clearly, my lord."

"The moment of the poisoning."

"I was watching closely."

"It's true!" he cries, leaping from the King's chair. "Come, some music," he shouts to the stewards nearby, who nod and leave to fulfill his command. "The recorders!" Hamlet calls after them. "For if the King can't enjoy comedy," he grins at Horatio, "perhaps he'd prefer a tuneful melody. Some music then."

Behind him, Rosencrantz and Guildenstern have come back to the hall.

"Might I have a word with you, my lord?" Guildenstern asks.

"A whole history, sir," Hamlet replies.

"The King, sir – "

"Yes, what about him?"

"Has gone to his room and he's just sick."

"With drink?"

"No, my lord, with anger!"

"You'd show yourself a wiser man if you reported this to his doctor, for if I were to prescribe something for what ails him, it would make his condition worse."

Guildenstern winces in frustration. "If you don't mind, my lord, could you keep to the matter at hand and stop wandering so wildly off topic."

"I'll see what I can do," Hamlet says, heaving a broadly sarcastic sigh. "What is it you wish to tell me?"

"The Queen your mother, in great distress, has sent me to see you."

"Welcome. Make yourself comfortable."

"No, please my lord, this kind of politeness isn't appropriate. If you would be good enough to give me a straight answer, then I will be able to carry out your mother's instructions. If not, with your permission I'll leave and my return to her will bring this errand to an end."

"Sir, I cannot."

"Cannot what, my lord?" Guildenstern asks, frustrated.

"Give you a straight answer. My mind's diseased. And so, sir, you'll have to help me find the answer you want, or rather my mother wants. But enough about that; back to the matter at hand. You say my mother – "

"Your mother," Rosencrantz chimes in, "says your behavior has left her amazed and bewildered."

"What a wonderful son who can actually astonish his mother! But is there nothing besides her amazement she wanted you to convey? Tell me."

"She would like to talk with you in her room before you go to bed."

"We can do that, were she ten times the mother she is. Is that everything?"

"My lord, you were my good friend once," Rosencrantz says, his voice tinged with sentiment.

"And still am, by these hands."

"Then what is causing you to behave like this? By refusing to be honest with your friends you risk being locked up in the madhouse."

Hamlet casts his eyes about the dark hall, making sure no one else can hear. He puts his mouth up to his friend's ear.

"Sir," he confides, "I've been robbed of my rightful role."

Rosencrantz frowns. "How can that be when the King has proclaimed you as the heir to his throne."

"Indeed, but while he rules in my father's stead, I must bide my time... Ah, here are the recorders!"

The Players come hurrying into the hall performing bright and cheerful tunes.

When Hamlet asks to see one, a player hands him an instrument. "To get back to you," he says to Guildenstern, "why do you keep trying to trick me, as though there's a trap into which you want me to fall."

"O my lord," Guildenstern replies, a guilty look on his face, "if I'm being too pushy it's only because I'm trying so hard to do my duty."

"I'm not sure I believe that. But never mind. Will you play this recorder for me?" He holds out the instrument.

"My lord, I cannot," Guildenstern says, shaking his head.

"Just give it a try."

"Believe me, I can't play."

"Come, I insist."

"I don't know the first thing about it, my lord."

"It's no different than lying. You cover the openings with your fingers and thumb, blow air into it with your mouth, and out come the sounds you want." He demonstrates. "Look, here are the stops where you put your fingers."

Hamlet forces the recorder into Guildenstern's hands.

"As I say, I don't know how it works. I don't have any skill, my lord."

"Then you must think very little of me," Hamlet tells him. "You enjoy playing me, you act as if you know how to work my stops, you keep trying to get something out of me, you play me from the low end of the scale to the high. There's so much music, such fine sound here in this little instrument, and yet you cannot get it to play. God, do you think I'm easier to be played than a recorder? Call me whatever instrument you wish, though you finger my frets, you can't play upon me. God bless you, sir," he says to Polonius, who has come to stand with a sheepish looking Guildenstern.

"My lord, the Queen would like to see you right away."

"Do you see that cloud up there that's shaped just like a camel?" Hamlet asks intently, gazing up and pointing to the darkness under the ceiling of the great hall, where smoke from the torches and the fireplace gathers.

"Indeed, I do," Polonius says, peering inquisitively upwards, "and it does look like a camel."

"Or perhaps a weasel."

"It seems to have the back of one."

"Or it could be a whale."

"Yes, a whale," Polonius agrees, uncertain as to where the game is leading.

His point made, Hamlet lowers his gaze and turns away. "Then I will come and see my mother right away." He looks in the direction of Horatio. "They force me to play the fool till it's almost unbearable," he says, heedless of the fact the others can hear.

Ready to leave, Polonius gestures for Hamlet to precede him but the Prince doesn't move.

"As I said, I will be there right away…"

"I will tell her so," Polonius says with a curt nod and hurries off.

"'Right away' is so easy to say," Hamlet murmurs. "Leave me, my friends," he says to Rosencrantz and Guildenstern.

Horatio lingers a moment then offers Hamlet a commiserating look – should he stay or go? Hamlet nods and smiles at his friend, who obliges by making for the door.

Alone by the light of the candles and the one torch left burning by the stage, Hamlet gazes into the surrounding darkness.

"It is the very time of night when witches lurk, when graveyard coffins open, breathing rank and putrid fumes into the world. Now could I drink a vat of steaming blood, and wreak such bitter havoc as the day would shudder to behold. So…I will go and meet my mother, but heart, stay mindful of affection. Help me to be cruel but not inhuman, my words like daggers but no worse – even if, in this, they are at odds with how I feel. Though what I say is vicious in attack, O heart, from murderous deeds, please hold me back."

Within his private chamber, the King advises Rosencrantz and Guildenstern of his plans.

"I don't like this at all, nor do I feel it's safe that in his madness he meanders where he likes. Therefore make yourselves ready. I'm sending you with commissions off to England right away and he will go along. As King I cannot risk the growing danger of his schemes."

"We will make the necessary preparations," Guildenstern assures the King. "It is a solemn, sacred duty to protect the many whose well-being must rely upon your Majesty."

"The private individual must, of course, protect himself from harm with all the strength of mind he can. But this holds true especially for that power who has so many depending on him for their welfare. The death of a King is not a lone event, but like a whirlpool draws what's nearby down into its depths – the way a massive carriage wheel set on the summit of the highest mountain might, ten thousand lesser creatures attaching to its spokes, so when it falls, even the smallest and most trivial of hangers-on are doomed to their destruction. Never did a King so much as sigh without his kingdom sighing too."

"Prepare yourselves promptly for the voyage if you would. Meantime, I will have the threat contained that runs too freely for my liking."

No sooner have the two friends left than Polonius scurries in to see the King.

"He's going to his mother's room, my lord. I'll station myself behind the Arras tapestry so I can hear what Hamlet says to her. I'm sure she will chastise him firmly, and as you so wisely said, it's vital that someone else besides his mother be there to listen in, mothers tending always to side with their natural born. Farewell, my lord. I'll come back before you go to bed and tell you what I know."

"Thanks, my dear lord."

The King sees Polonius out the door then moves to an adjoining room, a small chapel with chairs, benches and pews, and an altar where numerous candles are burning.

"What I have done is so rank and loathsome it smells to highest heaven. It has the mark of Cain upon it too – the murder of a brother. What makes me think that I can pray? As much as I would like to, my guilt outweighs by far the yearning I have to kneel, and like a man with double obligations, I pause in contemplation, unsure where I should first begin, and thus neglect them both. What if this killing hand were steeped up to the forearm with my brother's blood? Would there be enough rain in merciful heaven to cleanse it, and make the offending hand as white as snow again? What's the point of mercy, except to help us in the face of sin? And after all, in praying there's said to be a double power, whereby we ask not to be led into temptation, and forgiven if we are so led and trespass after all. I will look to heaven," he decides, stepping toward the altar. "My sin is in the past – though what could be a prayer that meets this present need? 'Forgive me for committing murder?' That cannot be, since I still possess the things for which I murdered in the first place – my crown, my Queen, my personal ambition. Can one be pardoned for a crime and still retain its profits? In the corrupt ways of the world, the guilty can have justice look the other way with bribing hands, and it's now becoming common for ill-got gains to buy the law's cooperation. But this is not so in heaven: there are no evasive tricks one can resort to; what we've done here is in full view there so all can see the truth, and we are called upon to present the evidence for our misdeeds, withholding not a thing. What then? What can one do? Repentance might work. But it might not. What can be done when there's not even the possibility of repentance? O wretched state, heart as black as death! My soul within a trap – the more it struggles to free itself, the more it becomes entangled. Help me angels, at least to make an effort. Bend, stubborn knees; let my heart lose its steel hardness and soften like the sinews of a newborn child. All may yet be well…"

He kneels in front of the altar, folds his hands and closes his eyes to begin praying, unaware that Hamlet is watching from the back of the chapel.

"I could do it now while he's praying – so easily. And I will," he declares as he takes out his sword. "And then he goes to heaven? And I have my revenge? Consider more carefully," he tells himself. "A villain kills my father, and for that reason I, his only son, kill that villain, thereby sending him to heaven – which is not revenge but a reward for what he's done. He killed my father while he was feasting and indulging openly in all his favorite pleasures; only heaven knows what that will mean when he makes his final account. As far as our earthly reckoning goes, it won't add up very well. Can I possibly have my vengeance if I kill him while he is busy confessing his sins, clearing his conscience and preparing to depart this life? No. Away, sword." He puts his weapon back in its sheath. "Find a worse moment than this: when he has passed out from drinking too much, when he's consumed with rage, panting with incestuous pleasure in bed, cursing his gambling losses – doing anything that offers him no hope of salvation. And I'll trip him so he falls with his back to heaven, so he's caught with his soul as damned and black as the hell to which he goes. My mother waits," Hamlet says, as if speaking to the King. "This praying but prolongs your evil days."

With the King suddenly getting to his feet, Hamlet slips out of the chapel.

"My words rise up," the King says uneasily, "but my thoughts remain below. Words without thoughts, to heaven, are but for show…"

Polonius takes a moment to catch his breath before guiding the anxious Queen toward a large woven tapestry hanging from the wall in her bedroom.

"He will be here any minute. Now, the point to hit home," he advises, "is that his behavior has become too outrageous to be tolerated – it's only through your Majesty's intervention he's been spared the brunt of other people's anger." He slips behind the tapestry but sticks his head out. "Remember, be blunt with him, my lady."

"I will, don't worry. Hide now, I hear him coming."

"Mother?"

Noticing the end of Polonius's cane sticking out from behind the tapestry, the Queen calls to him under her breath and the cane disappears from view just as Hamlet arrives.

"Now, mother. What's the matter?"

"Hamlet, you've greatly offended your father."

"Mother, you have greatly offended my father."

"Come, come, you answer with a foolish tongue."

"Go, go, you question with a wicked one."

"Hamlet!"

"What's the matter?"

"Have you forgotten who you're talking to?"

"Not at all. You are the Queen, your husband's brother's wife. And, though I wish it weren't so, you are also my mother."

"Well then," the Queen replies, offended by his insolence, "I'll go and get those who can make you talk properly."

She steps quickly around him, shaking off his hand when he attempts to hold her back.

"Come, come," Hamlet snaps, but then realizes she's on her way to the door. He rushes after her and catches her by the hair, which she has let down for the night. "You'll sit over here," he says sternly, leading her over to the writing table near the tapestry, "and go nowhere until I've let you see into your very heart and soul."

"Puh!" the Queen says dismissively, breaking away from him again.

This time Hamlet seizes her by the arms instead, bending one behind her back so hard that she cries out in pain. He pushes her fiercely across the room and shoves her violently down onto a chair beside the writing table. But she refuses to stay put, leaving Hamlet no choice but to take her by the throat as though he's going to strangle her if she doesn't sit down.

"What are you doing?" she gasps. "Do you want to kill me? Someone help!"

"Help, someone help!" Polonius's muffled yell comes from behind the tapestry.

"What's this?" Hamlet cries out when he sees someone moving behind the tapestry. He draws his sword, rushing at the wall. "A rat! Take the death you deserve – " He plunges his sword through the tapestry.

"No!" comes Polonius's forlorn cry, "you've slain me…"

"O, what have you done?" Beside herself with grief, the Queen reaches for the tapestry where the body of Polonius sinks slowly to the floor.

"Why don't *you* tell me," Hamlet replies. "Is it the King?"

He lifts the bottom of the tapestry only to see Polonius lying dead from a bloody wound to the chest.

"O what a reckless, bloody deed this is!"

"Bloody indeed. Almost as bad, good mother, as kill a King and marry his brother."

"Kill a King?"

"Yes, my lady, that's what I said – " He peers down at the lifeless Polonius. "You miserable, meddling fool…farewell. I mistook you for the King." He shakes his head in anger. "Fate's final lesson, old man: it's dangerous not minding your own business – "

Hamlet sees his mother pacing about, frantic with fear as much as grief.

"Stop wringing your hands. Calm down. Sit," he says, pointing nowhere in particular with his sword, "and I will wring your heart instead, provided it's still capable of feeling anything – if your debauchery hasn't sealed it off from the bounds of reason.

"What have I done," she pleads, "that you must rail against me so vehemently?"

"Such an act that puts grace and modesty to shame, makes a virtue of hypocrisy, wipes the blush off love's innocent face and sets a festering sore there instead, renders marriage vows as false as gamblers' promises – a deed that tears up the very contract of your soul, so 'good faith' is nothing but a meaningless pair of words. Heaven's livid face glares at the earth and all its elements with an air of mournful condemnation, horrified by what you have done."

"But, what act cries out so thunderously for judgment?" she asks again.

Hamlet grabs the chain around his neck, which holds a locket with a small picture of his father in it. He then plucks the cameo locket his mother wears around her neck and puts the two of them side-by-side.

"Look at these pictures," he begins, "portraits of two brothers." He forces her to look closely at his. "See what grace there was in this man's face? The curls of golden Apollo, the bearing of warrior Mars ready to threaten or command, his whole demeanor like the divine Mercury pausing briefly on a towering hill to reflect on the world at his feet – the image agreed upon by all the gods of what a man should be. This was your husband!"

He lets go of the locket and brings his mother's forward for her to see.

"Compare him with this man, who is your husband now – who spread like fungus and infected his healthy brother. Don't you have eyes? How could you leave the fair mountain pastures to live off such uncultivated land? Don't you have eyes? You can't call it love, for at your age the ecstasies of passion have subsided, become modest and conscious of what others say – and what would they say about going from this," he asks, holding up his locket, "to this?" He holds up hers. "You still have feelings, otherwise you wouldn't be as upset as you are now, but somehow they've been sealed away inside, because even madness wouldn't let you go so far – let you become so enthralled that you couldn't tell the difference between these two men. What devil tricked you into wearing his blindfold? You look but don't see, touch but don't feel, hear but don't comprehend, all sense gone except perhaps smell, though even in a weak moment no true sense would have left you like this. O shame, why won't you even blush? And rebellious Hell, if you can make a middle-aged woman lose all control of herself, decency will melt like wax over the flames of younger passion – but there should be no shame when desire overtakes them, since older and cooler feelings can burn as hot as all the rest when reason stoops to pandering to the will."

"O Hamlet, say no more! You force me to stare into my very soul where guilt is etched in marks so black they cannot be removed."

"How can that be," Hamlet asks, bearing down on her, "when you live between his sweat-soaked sheets, steeped in lust, whimpering while you make love in the filthy sty he uses for a bed."

She cowers before him, holding up her hands as he moves closer, the look on his face growing more menacing.

"No more! These words are like daggers to my ears! No more, sweet Hamlet."

"A murderer and a villain, a nobody who is not even a fraction of the man your first husband was, a parody of a King, a thief who grabbed an empire and all that goes with it – who stole his crown off a shelf and put it in his pocket – "

"No more, I can't bear it!" she protests, staggering backwards until she falls on her bed.

"A King made from rags and patches," Hamlet continues relentlessly, climbing on the bed and pinning her arms down. But he suddenly breaks off when he sees the ghost of his father watching from the other side of the room. "Angels protect me and hover nearby on guardian wings. What do you want, gracious lord?"

"My God, you're crazed," the Queen says, staring up at him.

"Did you not come to scold your tardy son," Hamlet asks the ghost, "who by wasting time and letting his feelings cool has failed to follow your express command? Tell me."

Don't forget. My appearance is but to sharpen your almost blunted purpose. Look how your mother recoils in horror. Put yourself in her place and try to understand what it is that torments her so – the weak suffer more in their imagination than do the strong.

The ghost's words slowly registering, Hamlet glances down at his mother. "How are you, my lady?" he asks, his voice softening, as if he's suddenly sensitive to what he has put her through.

"Better that I should ask how you are, staring into empty space and speaking to thin air. Your eyes are wild and frenzied, your hair mussed and standing on end as though it were coming to attention like sleeping soldiers jumping from their beds as the alarm sounds. O gentle son, sprinkle cool patience on the madness that is burning you up – what on earth are you looking at?"

In a trance, Hamlet slides off the bed and heads across the room. "On him," he tells his mother, "on him. His pale stare, the pained expression on his face, together with the wrongs he has suffered, would move stones to feel for him if they heard his story. – Don't look at me, spirit! For that pitiful sight distracts me from the vengeance I have sworn to seek – my actions lacking conviction would be driven by compassion instead of courage…"

"To whom are you saying these things?"

"Do you see nothing there?'

"Nothing at all…besides what is there."

"You heard no one?"

"No one but ourselves."

"But look there – look how it glides quietly away. My father, dressed in the clothes he wore when alive! Look, he's leaving through the door…"

Bewildered, the Queen regards the closed door to her room then turns and fastens her eyes on Hamlet.

"This is all in your mind. A figment of your imagination which madness cleverly makes you believe is really there."

"My pulse beats as evenly as yours with the rhythm of perfectly good health," he declares. "It is not madness that had me talking. You can put it to the test. Ask me what was said and I'll repeat myself word for word, something I couldn't do if I were mad, mother. For the love of grace, don't fool yourself into thinking it was my madness and not your wrongdoing that prompted me to say the things I have. That only creates a surface film on the festering sore, while gross corruption works invisibly within to deepen the infection. Confess your sins to heaven, repent the past and avoid what is to come; if you don't, sin spread over sin, like compost, thickens the weeds where they once were thin. Forgive me for harping on virtue like this. But when debauchery makes the world lax, virtue has to beg vice's pardon, bowing and scraping at times for permission to do wickedness some good."

"O Hamlet, you have cut my heart in two."

"Then throw away the worse half and live purely with the other. Good night," he says, turning away to reflect. "Mother, don't go to bed with my uncle later on. Make yourself seem virtuous, even if you're not. Though dull routine can take the excitement even out of our bad habits, it is a blessing in that the more we do good things, the more accustomed to them we become, as clothes feel comfortable the more we wear them. Refrain tonight, and that will make it easier for him to go without the next time, and the time after that. For a habit can change a facet of our character and control the devil that plagues us, or throw him out with amazing force." He watches her move so that she's sitting on the edge of the bed. "Once again, good night, and when you are ready to ask for repentance, I will be ready to ask for mine."

Hamlet goes and stands over the body of Polonius.

"For this lord here, I repent what I've done, except heaven has seen fit to punish me with doing this, and this man with having it done to him, making me the instrument of punishment and the punishment too. I will dispose of him and answer for the fact that I was the one who killed him. So, good night again." He bends down and rolls Polonius over. "In order to be kind, I've had to be cruel..."

Standing up, Hamlet walks back to his mother's bed. "Things have begun poorly," he declares matter-of-factly, "and worse lies ahead. But there is one more thing, good lady." He motions for his mother to get up so he can remove the bed spread, decorated with the royal coat of arms.

"What is that?"

"Under no circumstances do any of these: let his corpulent Highness take you to bed with him, pinch and tickle you where he likes to, call you his 'little pet' and in return for a few rank kisses and some fondling with his foul fingers, persuade you to reveal the truth, that I am not actually mad at all but merely acting that way. Don't tell him you felt he should know this, for who but a good Queen – beautiful, discreet and wise – would hide such serious business from her toad, her bat, her old tomcat? Why do that? No, my instincts tell me this calls for complete secrecy. Let the cat out of the bag, let the pigeons fly the coop, and like the ape who jumped into a cage just to see what it was like, you'll end up breaking your neck trying to get out."

"Believe me, if words are made from breath and breath gives them voice, I have no voice to breathe a word of what you've told me."

"I'm being sent to England, did you know?"

"Yes, but I'd forgotten. It has been decided."

"The royal letters are sealed and my two school friends, whom I trust as far as a pair of poisonous snakes, have orders to accompany me and lead me into some dangerous business. But so be it – what's more amusing than a man who steps in his own trap, gets blown up by the very bomb he's planting? Indeed, it would be rather strange if I weren't able to get one step ahead of them so they fall victim to the particular scheme they have hatched. It's always exhilarating when two things going in such different directions end up colliding head on."

The Queen watches grimly as Hamlet lays the bedspread out on the floor beside Polonius and rolls him onto it.

"This man will be sure to hasten my departure. I'll lug his carcass into the next room. Mother, a very good night to you." He takes two corners of the bedspread and prepares to leave. "This counselor to the King, such a silly, chattering fool during his life, now so still, so quiet, so grave. Come, sir, I'll drag this out, though not the way you used to. Good night, mother."

He drags Polonius over to the door and leaves. The Queen remains behind, noticing the old man's cane lying where it fell on the floor beside the tapestry....

4.1

Anxious to find out what went on between Hamlet and his mother, the King hurries into her bedroom, Rosencrantz and Guildenstern in tow. Gertrude is sitting on the edge of her bed, sobbing mournfully.

"Tell me what happened that has upset you so," the King says, a hand on his sword as he glances uneasily about the room. "Where is Hamlet?"

"Leave us for a few minutes, if you please," the Queen says to Rosencrantz and Guildenstern. Once they've left, she wipes her eyes with a handkerchief and takes a moment to regain her composure. "O, my lord, what I have witnessed tonight."

"Gertrude, how is Hamlet?"

"Mad as the sea when waves wrestle the storm wind to see who is mightier." She takes a breath before continuing. "In the throes of absolute madness, hearing something stir behind the tapestry, he drew his word, cried 'A rat, a rat' and in a raving frenzy killed the good old man in his hiding place." She takes the cane that belonged to Polonius and hands it to the King.

"O heinous deed!" the King declares, accepting the cane. "It would have been me if I had been there. As long as he is free he is a threat to all – you yourself, us, everyone. How on earth shall we deal with such a bloody act as this? The blame will be placed on us, for not having the foresight to deal with him sooner and keep him from being in the company of others. Yet it was our excessive concern that prevented us from determining what was best for him – as though he suffered from some dreaded disease we preferred not to divulge, thereby allowing it to get worse the longer it went untreated. But where is he now?"

"Disposing of the dead body, over which – in unmistakable madness – he weeps for what he has done," she lies.

"O Gertrude, come with me." He reaches out a hand and helps her stand up.

"We'll send him away first thing in the morning, and this horrible deed we will put on our best face to explain, and be extremely tactful about excusing. Guildenstern!" he calls, the two young men appearing promptly. "Friends, go and get help. Hamlet has killed Polonius in a fit of madness and has taken the body somewhere. Go and find him – humor him if necessary – and bring the body to the chapel as quickly as possible."

They rush out of the room, leaving the King consoling his wife.

"Come, Gertrude, we'll summon our most trusted friends and let them know how we intend to deal with what has so unfortunately taken place. That is the only way of avoiding blame when vicious rumors begin to fly, as they no doubt will. So come away. My heart is full of deep discomfort and dismay."

"Safely hidden away…"

Hamlet comes from a secret passageway off the library, turning the wall of books that disguises the entrance back to its normal position. But no sooner has he done so than he hears people shouting in the hall.

"Who's calling out my name?" He listens for a moment. "Of course, it's them," he scowls and takes a book from the closest shelf, just as Rosencrantz and Guildenstern barge into the library, a platoon of guards deploying throughout the room behind them.

"What have you done with the dead body, my lord?" Rosencrantz inquires.

"Mixed it with dust, his close relative now…"

"Tell us where it is so we can have it moved to the chapel where it belongs."

"Don't believe it."

"Believe what?"

He holds the book in front of his mouth so the guards can't hear him. "That I can keep your secrets and not my own. Besides, to be questioned by a sponge – what answer can the son of a King possibly give?"

"Do you take me for a sponge, my lord?" Rosencrantz asks, offended.

"That I do, sir, who soaks up the King's rich favor, rewards and residue of power. Although such servants do serve the King best in the end: he keeps them in the corner of his mouth – first to be chewed, but last to be swallowed. When he needs the information you've absorbed, he merely squeezes you and, Sponge, you are dry again."

"I don't quite understand that, my lord."

"I'm glad. Even foolish words are wasted on a fool."

"My lord, you must tell us where the body is and come with us to see the King."

"The body is with one King, but the other King is not with the body. The King is a thing – "

"A thing, my lord?" Guildenstern asks, frowning.

"Of no-thing. Take me to him."

The King is meanwhile conferring with his highest-ranking Lords in a council chamber. Seated at the long oak table, the grave Lords listen as Claudius briefs them on the situation.

"I have people searching for him and the body. It's extremely dangerous with him on the loose like this. Yet we mustn't bring down the strong arm of the law just yet. He's loved by the people, who of course judge by appearances and not hard facts. Thus they will react to whatever punishment is meted out, rather than the offence of which he is guilty. To keep the peace and at the same time maintain order, sending him away as we're doing will be perceived as the wisest move under the circumstances. After all, a disease which has become critical is only cured by applying a critical remedy."

The assembled Lords are acknowledging his point with sage nods when Rosencrantz and Guildenstern arrive, attended by several guards, but not Hamlet.

"Well?" the King demands.

"My lord," Rosencrantz replies, "we can't find out from him where he's hidden the body."

"And where is he?"

"We have him under guard and await your instructions."

"Bring him in."

Rosencrantz nods. "Ho!" he calls to the guards outside. "Bring in the Prince."

Hamlet, an amused smirk on his face, is led into the room closely escorted by six guards. Before signaling the guards to leave, the King throws Rosencrantz a questioning glance; he holds up Hamlet's sword and dagger. Satisfied, the King dismisses the guards and confronts Hamlet.

"Where is Polonius, Hamlet?" he begins sternly.

"At supper."

"At supper? Where?"

"Not a place where he's eating, but where he's being eaten. A crafty mob of maggot worms is feasting on him as we speak. The wormy maggot is the King of eaters as I'm sure you know, my lord: we fatten our animals in order to fatten ourselves, and we fatten ourselves for the worms. The fat King and the lean beggar are just two different courses as far as they're concerned – two dishes served at the same meal. And that's that."

The King can only shake his head in frustration. "Alas," he sighs wearily, and looks apprehensively at the high Lords, who are confused, to say the least.

"A man may fish with the worm that ate a King," Hamlet carries on, "or eat the fish that fed on the worm."

"What is that supposed to mean?"

"Just that a King can pass through the guts of a beggar."

"Where is Polonius?" Claudius demands once more.

"In heaven. Send someone there to check. If your messenger can't locate him, look for him in the other place yourself. However, if you don't manage to find him before the end of the month, your nose will tell you where he is as you go up the rear stairs, behind the lobby."

"Have the guards go and look for him there," the King instructs Guildenstern.

"He'll be waiting for you!" Hamlet calls after his friend.

"Hamlet, for your own protection – which concerns us as much as what you've done – it's imperative that you be sent away as soon as possible. Therefore get prepared, a ship has been made ready, a favorable wind is blowing, your companions waiting, and everything is arranged for the trip to England."

He motions some guards back into the room

"For England?"

"Yes, Hamlet."

"Good."

"Yes it is, if you knew our intentions," the King says.

"I see an angel that sees them," Hamlet replies with a wry grin. "But come, it's off to England. Farewell dear mother."

The Lords sitting around the table raise their eyes.

"Your loving father, Hamlet," the King corrects him.

"My mother. Father and mother are man and wife, man and wife are one. Which makes you my mother. To England!" he shouts joyfully as he's led from the room.

The high Lords rise and prepare to leave.

"Stay close to him," the King advises Rosencrantz. "See that he gets on board right away. Don't let him linger, for any reason. I want him long gone by tomorrow night. Everything has been taken care of so get moving now, and remember, time is of the essence."

Rosencrantz and the Lords bow and depart.

Moving to the window, the King gazes out at the moonlit sea.

"England, if you value my friendship at its proper worth – as my great power should serve to remind you, the wounds inflicted by Danish arms yet red and raw, for which you freely pay your homage fees – you will not disregard the request I've disclosed to you in my letters to effect the immediate death of Hamlet. Do it, England. For he rages inside me like a fever, which only you can cure. Until I know it is done, among my many fortunes joy will not count as one…"

———— ♛ ————

Shortly after dawn, the Norwegian army is breaking camp on a wide, mist-covered field, taking down tents, dousing fires, saddling horses and making their way over to the road for the morning march to begin. It's a chilly morning, the breath of man and beast alike steaming in the frosty air.

Surrounded by soldiers in battle-dress and standard-bearers flying the red royal colors, Fortinbras, nephew of the Norwegian King, issues orders to one of his officers.

"Go, captain, and convey greetings to the Danish King from me. Tell him Fortinbras requests permission for his armies to pass through the kingdom as was agreed. Inform him as well that if his Majesty would like to speak with me, I would be pleased to present myself in person."

"I will do so, my lord."

"Carry on then…"

Mounting his horse, the captain rejoins his troops, however the morning mist is still too thick to ride cross-country so the captain and his men head for the nearby road…

Rosencrantz, Guildenstern and Hamlet, accompanied by a military escort flying the blue-and-white banners of the Danish King, get down off their horses when the Norwegian troops come into view, officers of the foreign battalions instructing their men to make way so the royal party can pass unimpeded. Soon the captain dispatched by Fortinbras approaches Hamlet and his two friends.

"Good sir, whose forces are these?" Hamlet inquires.

"They are from Norway, sir."

"Where are they headed, if I may ask?"

"Toward some part of Poland."

"Who commands them, sir?"

"Fortinbras, nephew to the Norwegian King."

"Are they going against Poland's main force or the frontier garrisons?

"To be quite honest, and without exaggerating, we're to take a small tract of land whose only value is symbolic. If they paid me one hundred dollars – one hundred – I wouldn't claim it for myself. The worst of it is, it wouldn't bring us or Poland much more than that if it were sold outright.

"Surely the Poles won't bother defending it then."

"Oh, it already has a full garrison guarding it."

"Two thousand lives and twenty-thousand ducats wouldn't be enough to settle a matter this trivial," Hamlet says bitterly. "This is the wretched abscess of wealth and peace, which swells until it breaks inside a man so there's no apparent cause of death. I am grateful, sir. Thank you."

"Goodbye, sir."

"We'd better get moving, my lord," Rosencrantz says to Hamlet, "if you don't mind."

He and Guildenstern get back on their horses, but Hamlet hesitates, peering into the mist-cloaked field as if he sees something. He drops his horse's reins and walks slowly into the field, Guildenstern moving to dismount and go after him, but Rosencrantz puts out a hand to stop him.

In a matter of moments Hamlet finds himself lost in the clouds of swirling mist. He turns one way and then the other, unable to see more than a few feet in front of him. At one point he is sure he glimpses his armor-clad father just up ahead. He runs to the place, but there is nothing except a wall of mist. Finally, he stops moving and stares off...

"How all events are turning now against me, asking why it is my vengeful spirit falters... What is a man if his chief purpose in life is but to eat and sleep: an animal, at best. Surely he who gave us the capacity for memory as well as the power to envision the future, didn't want to see these gifts of thought and reason fade away unused. Whether it were as simple as forgetting to do what I said, or cowardice and doubt arising from too much thinking about it – thinking which, if it were quartered, would be one part courage and three parts cowardice – I don't know why I still go through life telling myself 'This is something that I must do,' when I have the cause, the will, the strength and the means to have already done it.

"Examples so alike are right before my eyes and should inspire me

– look at the size and might of this army, led by an inexperienced young Prince, whose spirit, charged with confidence and zeal, just laughs in the face of the unknown, pitting himself life and limb against all that fate, death and danger dare him to overcome, and for something that in the end has so little value. Perhaps the truly great are not those who fight for the greater causes, but those who will fight for lesser ones when a principle is at stake. Where does that leave me then, who has had a father killed, a mother dishonored, the pleading of feeling, the arguments of reason urging me fast to do something, and yet I don't? While to my shame I see twenty-thousand men marching toward imminent death on a general's whim and with no prospect of glory – the way they'd head off to bed – to contest a piece of land which isn't big enough for the two armies to begin with, let alone their bodies when they need burying. O, from this moment on my thoughts be bloody or no longer worth –"

Rosencrantz has come up behind and put a hand on Hamlet's shoulder. The Prince nods but keeps his eyes front, peering into the mist as if he's still expecting to see someone....

Looking wan and tired from her sleepless night, the Queen is in a castle room with Horatio and a gentleman from her household staff.

"I won't speak with her," the Queen says firmly.

"She's adamant, my lady. Distraught. Even, I would say, to be pitied."

"What does she want?"

The gentleman shrugs. "She mentions her father a great deal, says she hears deceivers lurking all about, then she begins coughing and beating her chest, shrieking harshly at the air as she mumbles mysterious phrases that make little sense. It's mostly gibberish from the sounds of it yet the words are so strangely strung together it leaves one with a feeling she's actually trying to say something. She starts off clearly each time, but soon stumbles over her words, winking, nodding to herself, waving her hands as if she's expressing deep unhappiness, though one can't say for sure."

Horatio turns away from the window and approaches the Queen. "It would be a good idea to speak with her. She could spark nasty rumors among the gossip-hungry."

"Let her come in," the Queen says, after considering Horatio's advice, and the gentleman goes quickly out the door.

"In my desperation," she murmurs to herself, "as is the case after doing wrong, even the smallest thing seems to foretell impending disaster. Guilt breeds such terrible fear and suspicion it gives itself away in trying not to let them show."

A demented expression on her face, her eyes red from weeping, Ophelia sweeps into the room and prances up to the Queen. "Where is the beauteous Majesty of Denmark?" she asks in a rasping voice.

"How are you Ophelia?"

"*'How would I your true love know,'*" she sings, "*'from someone else's when we meet? Likely by his grand cocked hat, by the sandals on his feet.'*"

"Indeed, sweet lady, but what do you mean with a song like this?"

"What did you say? No, please, just listen. *'He is dead and gone lady, I am all alone; by his head the soft green grass, by his heels the granite stone.'* Oh who?"

"Please, Ophelia," the Queen says with compassion.

"Please yourself, just listen. *'White his death shroud, white as snow?'*"

The King appears at the door of the room.

"*– covered with sweet flowers, which did not weep on the way to the grave, with true-love's tearful showers.'*"

"How are you pretty lady?" the King asks, stepping into the room.

"Well, God reward you. They say the owl was once a baker's daughter. Lord, how we can know what we are yet not what we will become. God be at your table," she says, bowing to him.

"Mourning her father," the King says to the Queen and Horatio.

"Please let's not have words like that, though when they ask you what it means, tell them this. *'Tomorrow is St. Valentine's Day, when the sun begins to shine; and I a maiden at your window, want you for my Valentine. Then up he rose and donned his clothes, he opened wide his chamber door, let in the maiden who left a maiden no more.'*"

"Pretty Ophelia? "

"Oh sir, without an oath, I'll end it off right now. *'By Jesus and sweet charity, alas and oh what shame; young men do it if they come to it, by cock they are to blame. Said she, 'Before you took me to your bed, you promised we'd be wed.' ' And would be, swear I by the sun, if you had not to my bed come.'''*

"How long has she been this way?" the King asks, looking to Horatio.

"I hope all will end up well," Ophelia blurts by way of an answer. "We must be patient. Yet I have no choice but to weep when I think how they laid him down in the cold, cold ground. My brother shall hear of it. And so I thank you for your gentle help. Come. Make ready my coach. Good night, ladies, good night. Sweet ladies all, good night, good night…"

She gathers the folds of her dress, whisks past the Queen and rushes from the room.

"Follow her closely," the King tells Horatio. "Don't let her out of your sight," he says emphatically. He deliberates a moment before turning to the Queen. "What a toll her father's death is taking; just look what it has done… O Gertrude, Gertrude, when sorrows come they don't inflict themselves singly but in droves. First her father is killed; next, your son is sent away, though what he did left us no choice in the matter; the people are growing more agitated every hour, confused and suspicious in their opinions about good Polonius's death – whom we have foolishly chosen to bury quickly and in secret; poor Ophelia struggles to keep her sanity and very sense of self which elevates us above the animals; last but not least her brother has, unknown to many, returned from France. He can think of nothing except this troubling turn of events, keeping himself out of the public eye, although he's being given a steady stream of vicious rumors and accusations about the actual circumstances of his father's death, gossips needing fuel to feed their slanderous fires as they take it upon themselves to suggest it was all my fault. O my dear Gertrude, it feels like the scattering shot from cannon fire: I am taking hits from all sides.

Suddenly a loud commotion can be heard in the hall outside the room.

"What's going on?" the Queen asks her husband.

"Attendants! Where are my Swiss guards? See that they're deployed!"

A messenger knocks and enters without waiting for an answer. "Save yourself, my lord," he says frantically. "A tidal wave crashes past the break wall and surges inland with nowhere near the force young Laertes and a band of rebel followers did when they overpowered your officers a few moments ago. The crowd are calling him 'leader' and, as if they want to start a new society – wiping out the past and the valued customs and traditions that embody our principles – they cry 'We want Laertes! Make Laertes King.' They cheer and applaud wildly, and throw their hats in the air – 'Laertes shall be King, Laertes shall be King.'"

"How keenly they follow the wrong trail," the Queen remarks. "You're after the wrong person you false Danish dogs!" she cries defiantly over the din of shouts and metal clanging against metal as the King's guards work to quell a scuffle.

"They're trying to break in?" the King cries, just as the door to the room flies open and Laertes, backed by a dozen followers, forces his way past the King's guards.

"Where is the King?" he demands, perspiring and out of breath, then sees Claudius on the other side of the room. "Sirs, wait for me outside," he orders his men.

"No, we're staying, sir," they protest.

"Give me a moment alone here. Please"

"Right, then," they grumble and reluctantly retreat to the hall.

When they've left, Laertes confronts Claudius.

"Give me my father you base villain!" he shouts in anguish and leaps at the King, the Queen throwing herself between him and her husband.

"Calm down, good Laertes," she says with firmness and affection, restraining him.

"If there's a drop that's calm in my blood it not only calls me bastard and mocks my father for having an unfaithful wife, but denounces my all too faithful mother as nothing but a whore."

"Laertes, what is it that has you up in arms like this? Let him go,

Gertrude. Don't worry – Kings are protected by a divine barrier that treason can peer over when it likes but do nothing about crossing. Tell me, Laertes, why are you so incensed at me? – Let him go, Gertrude. It's all right. – Answer me, Laertes."

"Where is my father?"

"Dead."

"But not by his Majesty," the Queen puts in.

"Let him ask me what he likes."

"How did he die? And I warn you I won't be trifled with, loyalty be damned – I can side with the blackest devil and not give it a second thought! Hurl conscience and divine forgiveness to the bottomless pit because I don't fear damnation in the least. I'm resolved on this point especially: neither this world nor the next means anything to me so long as I can, in spite of everything else, have complete revenge for my father's death."

"Can nothing stop you?"

"Nothing and no one. I will only stop when I have accomplished what I set out to do. As to the means at my disposal, I have very little, but I will make sure it goes a good long way."

"Good Laertes, if you're set on finding out what really happened to your father, does that mean you'll take down friends and foes alike if they appear to be standing in your way? Sweep the table clean, so to speak, and have revenge at all costs?"

"It's only enemies I'm after."

"Shouldn't you find out who they are first?"

Laertes considers the King's comment.

"I will gladly open my arms to his friends and let them nourish memories of him through me," he tells the King.

"Why, now you're talking like a good son and true gentleman. You should know, Laertes, that not only am I guiltless of your father's death, I am grief-stricken about it?"

There is more noise out in the hall and then the sound of Ophelia singing amid the raised voices.

"Let her come in," the King calls.

"Whose voice is that?" Laertes asks uneasily.

The guards and Laertes's men make way as Ophelia steps delicately into the room, her eyes darting looks everywhere but at people.

"O heat, dry up all conceptions in my brain! Tears laden with salt burn the sight from my eyes. In heaven's name, I swear someone will pay for this madness and so much more. O rose of May! Dear child – kind sister – sweet Ophelia – how is it possible that a young girl's hold on life can be as fragile as an old man's? Love perfects nature, and when it's perfect it sends some token of itself to the grave, to follow the thing it loves…"

"*'They laid him bare-faced on the coffin,'*" Ophelia sings softly. "'*Her tears the earth below did soften'*– farewell my dove."

"If you still had your wits about you," Laertes says gently to his sister, "and pleaded with me to have revenge on someone who had hurt you, it wouldn't have moved me the way this does."

"You must sing '*In the ground in the ground*' and you '*Call him in-the-ground, oh.*' How the spinning wheel does it!" She glances at the King. "It was the lying lover who stole his master's daughter," she says accusingly.

"This nonsense has something to it," Laertes says hopefully.

"There's rosemary," Ophelia says, tenderly giving her brother an imaginary flower. "That's for remembrance – pray you, love, remember. And there's pansies," she says, approaching the Queen, "that's for thoughts." She has the Queen put out a hand to receive her invisible flowers.

"There's a lesson in this madness," Laertes says, "since thought and memory go together."

"There's fennel for you, and columbines," she tells her brother and places more imaginary herbs in his hand before gliding over to the King. "There's rue for you," she says, her stare so upsetting he has to look away. "And here's some for me. We call it 'herb of grace' on Sundays." She glances at the King and frowns. "You must wear rue with distinction," she says, mildly scolding him. Reaching up, she adjusts her imaginary flowers on his head. "There's a daisy too. I would give you some violets, but they all withered when my father died. They say he went peacefully. '*For bonny sweet Robin is all my joy,'*" she sings.

"She makes misery, suffering and sorrow – even her most tortured feelings – into things of grace and beauty," Laertes laments.

"*'And will he ever come again?'*" she resumes singing. "*'And will he ever come again? No, no, he is dead. Go to your own death bed – he will never come again. His beard was white as snow. His hair still golden blond. And so we moan in vain, for he is gone, he is gone, he is gone.'* And so, all goodly souls, goodbye..."

Singing quietly to herself, she dances away to the door, and goes out.

Laertes lets out a suffering moan. "Did you behold that?" he demands in agony.

"Laertes, let me share your grief with you," the King says consolingly. "Go off and select a group of your most trusted friends and let them judge between you and me. If they find me blatantly guilty or responsible in the slightest degree for what happened to your father, then I will forfeit my kingdom, my crown, my life and everything that is mine in order for you to find satisfaction. But if not, I ask you to exonerate me of any wrongdoing and work together with me to make sure you find the peace of mind you're looking for."

"Very well, but I will need to know how he died, details of your secret funeral – why no stone was placed over the grave, no crossed swords or coats-of-arms displayed outside his tomb, no last rites performed or funeral ceremony held – things which clamor to be explained, and so I call them into question."

"You are right to do so, and let the sword of justice fall on the guilty. Come along with me..."

Books spread out on a long wooden table in the library where he is working, Horatio has stopped writing to deal with a servant who is waiting somewhat anxiously for an answer.

"These people who wish to speak with me, who are they?" he asks the servant.

"Sailors, sir. They say they have some letters for you."

Horatio deliberates a moment. "Show them in," he says, but after the servant leaves he continues to ruminate. "Who on earth would be sending something to me?" he wonders out loud, until a possibility presents itself. "Except Hamlet..." he murmurs uneasily. He puts down his quill pen and gets up from the wooden table just as the servant ushers three sailors into the library.

"God bless you, sir," says the sailor spokesman.

"May he bless you too," Horatio replies.

"Here's hoping he does, sir, if it please him." He turns to one of the others. The sailor hands over a folded and wax-sealed piece of paper. "This is a letter for you, sir. It came from the ambassador who was on his way to England – if your name is Horatio, that is, which I'm led to believe it is."

Nodding, Horatio accepts the letter and opens it quickly.

"'Horatio, after you've read this, see that the King receives these fellows. They have letters for him also. We were barely two days at sea when pirates began to pursue us. Too slow to escape them, we were forced to fight, and during the grappling I boarded their ship unobserved, which made me their one and only prisoner when they broke away and sailed off. They have treated me as shrewd mercenaries should: sparing my life provided I do them a favor. Make sure the King sees the letters I've sent then join me as soon as you possibly can. I have things to tell you which you will find astounding, though that's putting matters lightly. These good men will bring you to my hiding place. Rosencrantz and Guildenstern continue on their way to England; I have much to tell you about them also. Farewell. He you know is yours, Hamlet.'"

Horatio refolds the letter and puts it into the leather bag he has with him at the table. He tucks his own papers rapidly into the bag, closes it up and, slipping the carrying strap over his shoulder, makes for the door.

"Come with me and we'll see your letters are delivered, the speedier the better, so you can take me to the man who gave them to you."

The King leads Laertes into the room commemorating the history of Denmark's royal family: numerous suits of metal armor stand on display and royal shields with colorful coats-of-arms and shining ceremonial swords are arranged in racks along the walls. Off-limits to anyone besides blood relatives of the King, Laertes is taken aback at the sight of so much ancestral history.

"Now that you've been made aware of the facts," the King explains, "and heard my innocence confirmed with your own ears, you must trust me as a friend when I tell you the man who killed your father was after me as well."

"So it appears. But just the same, tell me why you didn't do anything in reaction to these deeds of his, which were serious as well as criminal enough to warrant the most severe penalty – especially when, with your personal safety and political stability at stake, along with so much else, you had every reason to do so?"

"Two particular reasons, which to you may not seem to have much bearing on the situation, but for me have everything to do with it. The Queen his mother dotes upon him, and frankly – whether it's a blessing or a curse – she is such a part of my very heart and soul that I can't do a thing without first considering the impact it will have on her. The other reason I can't publicly hold him to account is the enormous affection the common people have for him. Their adoration is so great his popularity works like a fast running stream: smoothing the rough, unseemly aspects of everything he does so in some uncanny way they become shiny, eye-catching stones and his faults the most noble virtues. Thus any accusations I make, like arrows too light for a strong wind, come back to hit me rather than their intended target."

"Nevertheless, I have lost a noble father," Laertes says bitterly, "and have a sister driven into desperate straits – a sister who, prior to this, had that kind of perfection about her that has been revered throughout the ages." He examines a rack of long swords, the ornate handles and silver blades shining in the candlelight. "But my revenge will come," he declares solemnly.

"Don't lose sleep over that, nor think for a single minute we are made of such flimsy stuff as to let ourselves be threatened merely for someone's amusement. You will shortly hear more about this.

However, for now, accept that I loved your father as I love myself. Knowing this, I hope you can set your mind to thinking about – "

A firm knock comes at the door. When the King opens up it's a messenger holding out several letters. "These are for your Majesty, this one is for the Queen."

The King looks at the writing and recognizes it immediately.

"From Hamlet!" he exclaims. "Who brought them?"

"Some sailors, my lord. I didn't see the men myself. These were given to me by Claudio, who was the first to receive them."

"Laertes, you shall hear what they say. – Leave us," he says to the messenger, and when the man is gone the King opens the letter addressed to him.

"'*Your high and mighty Majesty,*" he reads, "*this is to let you know that I have been put ashore in your kingdom, naked you might say, without resources of any kind. Tomorrow I shall ask for an audience with your Kingly person and, with your permission, I shall try to explain my sudden and strange return. Hamlet.*'" Flustered and perturbed, he passes the letter to Laertes. "What could this possibly mean? Have all the others come back as well, or is this a hoax, some sort of trick?"

Laertes looks over the letter. "Do you recognize the handwriting?"

The King nods. "It is Hamlet's." He takes the letter back. "'Naked' – and in his post script he adds 'alone.' What do you make of that?" he asks Laertes.

"I have no idea, my lord – but let him come. It makes my agony more bearable when I think of telling him to his face 'Now it's your turn to die.'"

"If this is true, Laertes," the King says, holding up Hamlet's letter, "and there's as much reason to think that it is as it isn't, will you do what I ask you to?"

"Yes, my lord, just as long as you don't ask me to make peace with him."

The King shakes his head. "On the contrary, I'll help you make peace with yourself. If he has abandoned his voyage and returned with no intention of leaving again, I will convince him to accept a challenge that I've had in mind for some time, one which he can't help but fail, his death occurring in such a way there won't be the slightest whiff of blame, and even his mother will construe what happens as purely accidental."

"My lord, I will gladly do whatever you ask, especially if things are so arranged that I am the instrument of his destruction."

"That is what I am considering. You see, while you were living in France people talked about you from time to time – and were often overheard by Hamlet – as having a skill at which you shine. Among the various talents people raved about, none provoked Hamlet's jealousy as much as that, though to my mind it's the least impressive of your qualities."

"What skill are you thinking of, my lord?"

"A little light-heartedness, an attractive feature in young people, but quite necessary, too, for a casual, carefree style is as appropriate for them as sable robes and distinguished garments are for their elders when they wish to convey dignity and prosperity. In any event, two months ago there was a gentleman here from Normandy – I've seen for myself and fought against the French and they are splendid horsemen – but this gallant young man was an equestrian marvel. He looked like he was molded into the saddle, getting his animal to perform such intricate maneuvers that he and his horse seemed to occupy one body: half man, half beast. He so surpassed my expectations that any feats or tricks I could possibly dream up, fell far short of what he seemed capable of doing."

"From Normandy you said?"

"Normandy, yes."

"It must have been Lamord."

"That's the fellow."

"I know him well. He's his country's outstanding rider – a national treasure."

"He confessed to having the utmost admiration for you, and spoke in the most glowing terms of your skill and artful style as a swordsman – especially with the rapier – declaring that if you ever met your equal it would surely be something to see. He swore that French fencers were no match for your agility, precise targeting and shrewd defensive tactics. His testimonial made Hamlet so envious he couldn't stop talking about how much he was looking forward to you returning from France, just so he could fence with you. Now, out of this – "

"What out of this, my lord?"

The King gives him a questioning look.

"Was your father dear to you, Laertes? Or are you one of those whose face is the picture of sorrow while the heart has no such feeling?"

"Why would ask me that?" Laertes demands, offended.

"Not that I think for a moment you did not love your father, but I know that love is created in time, and experience has shown that time causes the sparks to fade and the fire to burn down. Within the very flame of love there is that which can extinguish it, a flaw in the wick, if you will, that snuffs it out. Nothing can maintain the same degree of goodness forever, for goodness, swelling to excess, dies from too much of itself. What we want to do, we should do when we have a mind to, otherwise 'I want to' changes and diminishes, encounters as many delays as there are excuses we can make, hands to hold us back, things which come along by accident, turning 'I ought to' into a wistful sigh, easing your conscience somewhat because you remain justified, but burdening you with guilt just the same because you can't make yourself take action. – To the heart of the matter: Hamlet has returned. What would you be willing to do to show that you are not just the son of Polonius in name only?"

"I'd slit his throat in church."

"Indeed, no place should provide refuge for a murderer; there should be no boundaries when it comes to revenge. Therefore, good Laertes, if you wish to do this, stay in your room for now. Hamlet, having come back, will hear that you are returned as well. We'll see that enough people acclaim your exceptional skills to double the luster of what the Frenchman said about you. That will have him request a match between the two of you, with bets placed on the outcome. He, being the unsuspecting kind, well mannered and above conniving, won't bother checking the foils beforehand, so that you can easily – or with a little shuffling – choose the sword whose tip is uncapped, and with a treacherous thrust at the first opportunity, you can repay him for what he did to your father."

"I will do it, and to that purpose poison my sword as well."

The King fixes Laertes with an inquiring frown.

"I purchased a small jar of ointment from a traveling doctor who deals in potions and poisons. This one is so lethal a mere scratch from a blade dipped in the mixture, despite the best of remedies and cures miraculous, is deadly. I'll smear the poison on the point of my foil. Then, even if I but slightly graze him during the contest, he is sure to die."

"Let's think this through carefully, considering the best possible way and the most opportune time to carry out our scheme. For if there's a chance that we could fail, and our plot exposed because our plan was badly executed, then it's best we not try in the first place. We should therefore have a back-up or secondary plan in case the first goes awry. Now, let me see…we'll be putting down serious wagers on your respective skills – what about this: when in the midst of fighting you're hot and thirsty from all the exertion – you should make the fighting as intense as possible with that in mind – and Hamlet asks for a drink, I'll have a goblet filled and ready, from which one sip will do what we want it to, if by chance he's avoided the tip of your sword up to that point. – Wait, what's that noise?"

He hurries over and listens at the door, opens quickly and admits the Queen. Looking shaken, her cheeks are wet with tears. "One tragedy comes right on the heels of another," she says through her sobs. But checks herself when she sees Laertes standing near the collection of swords. "Your sister," she offers quietly, "is drowned."

"Drowned? What do you mean?" he cries.

"There is a willow tree that grows from the bank out over the brook, its silvery leaves reflecting in the stream below. Ophelia went there and made beautiful garlands from the flowers growing nearby: yellow-cups, nettle fringe, daisy-whites and purple orchids – for which shepherds have a crude name, though young girls call them 'dead men's fingers.' She climbed up to drape her flower chains on the overhanging boughs, but, as if to spite her, a branch broke…which sent her, along with her flowers, into the water below. Her clothes, spread out on the surface of the water, kept her afloat mermaid-like as she sang songs from her childhood, oblivious to the danger she was in, or as if she felt herself at home, like one of the water's natural inhabitants. But it wasn't long before the clothes, saturated with water, pulled the poor thing away from her melodious singing and down to a muddy death."

Stunned and grief-stricken, Laertes lowers his head.

"You've had too much with water, Ophelia," he mourns, his voice shaking, "and so I'll hold back my tears." He struggles to maintain his composure. "Though it is the way of the world," he says, letting out a breath. "Nature taking its course. What does shame matter at a time like this – " But a moment later, overcome with emotion, he breaks down. " – Ophelia…"

The Queen comes over and holds him until his sobbing subsides. Uncomfortable, the King looks away…

Laertes slips from the arms of the Queen suddenly and begins speaking. "I have a fiery speech raging inside that would blaze hard and hot," he says defiantly, "if only the flames weren't being doused by these foolish tears; when they stop the woman will be out – "

In a swift movement he takes one of the ancient swords from the rack.

"Adieu, my lord," he says decisively and races out the door before the King can stop him.

"We have to watch him, Gertrude. It was all I could do to calm his anger earlier. This could well ignite it once again. Come – "

In the churchyard cemetery, a gravedigger and his young partner have put down their shovels while they rest on the mound of earth heaped up beside the nearly dug grave.

"Is it going to be a Christian burial after she took her own life?" the gravedigger wonders.

"I told you it would be," his partner says slowly. "So we'd better get this done. The coroner's been over the body and ruled a Christian burial."

"How can that be, unless she drowned herself in her own defense."

"I guess that's what they decided."

"It must be *se offendendo* then; can't be anything else."

"*Say* what?"

"*Off-en-den-do*," he repeats so his partner can understand. "But here's the point: if I drown myself knowingly, you have to consider that an act, and an act has three parts to it – there's to act, to do, and to perform; *eargo*, she drowned herself knowingly."

"But then Mister Delver – "

"Let me finish." He raises his hands to demonstrate. "Here lies the water," he gestures off to his right. His partner follows the movement of the gravedigger's hands.

"And here stands the person," he says, pointing off to the left. "All right?" His partner nods. "If *this* person, goes to *this* water and drowns himself, it is, willy-nilly, a drowning. Agreed?" His partner nods again. "Where at, if *this* water comes to *this* person and drowns him, then he didn't drown himself. *Eargo*, he who's not guilty of his own death doesn't shorten his own life."

The gravedigger's partner scratches his head. "Is this the law?"

"Sure it is," the gravedigger says. "It's law the coroners use when they do their ing-quests."

"Know what I think? If she hadn't been a gentlewoman she wouldn't be getting Christian burial."

"That's true. And greater's the pity that well born folk get to drown or hang themselves more than the rest of us good Christian souls. The only real gentlemen are the diggers who work the gardens, the ditches, the graves – since they follow in ancient Adam's footsteps."

"Was he a gentleman?"

"First with a coat of arms."

"Why, he didn't have arms."

"What are you, a heathen? Don't you know the Bible? The Bible says 'Adam digged.' How could he dig without arms? And another question. If you don't give me a straight answer, say your prayers and – "

"Go ahead," his partner says eagerly.

Not one to be rushed, the gravedigger frowns at his partner.

"Who builds things stronger than the stone mason, the shipwright or the carpenter?"

Up on his feet because he knows this one, the partner answers the riddle. "The gallows-maker, because what he builds outlasts a thousand customers!"

"That's a good one," the gravedigger chuckles. "The gallows is good. But – "

His partner abruptly stops laughing.

" – Why is it good?" the gravedigger asks and immediately answers his own question. "Because it does good to those who've done bad. Now, it's not the best thing for you to say a gallows is built stronger than a church; *eargo*, the gallows may make *you* one of its customers. Let's get to it. Come on."

Trying to remember if he said anything about a church, the partner picks up his spade and joins the digger in the grave.

They work in silence for a few minutes, but the partner hasn't stopped thinking about the gravedigger's riddle.

"Who builds stronger than a stone mason, a shipwright or a

carpenter?" he asks, putting the riddle again.

The gravedigger smiles. "All right, tell me and then give your brains a rest."

"I'll tell you," he declares, but continues to ponder.

"Go ahead."

"Well. It could be…" He hesitates, and then his face falls.

"Stop wracking your brains for now. You won't make a donkey go faster by beating it. Next time somebody asks you the riddle, just say 'A grave-maker. The houses he makes last till doomsday.'"

The partner stares at the gravedigger, puzzling over the answer.

"Here," the gravedigger says, taking a coin from his pants' pocket. "Go for a walk over to Vaughan's tavern and fetch me a bottle of ale."

The partner puts down his shovel, climbs from the grave and ambles off through the churchyard, leaving the gravedigger to work alone, singing as he digs.

"'*In youth when I did love, did love, I thought it very sweet, I did: to shorten the time, I worked as hard as any man could. Oh I thought there was nothing so good…*'"

His shovel hitting something in the ground, he stoops and comes up with a skull, which he tosses onto the dirt mound beside the grave. Not going to stay, the skull rolls right back down and tumbles into the hole. The digger picks it up, throws it in another direction, and resumes singing, unaware that Hamlet and Horatio have been watching.

"Has this fellow no feeling for what he's doing if he can sing while digging a grave?" Hamlet asks.

"He's so accustomed to it, he probably doesn't give it a second thought."

"It's true what they say about people who don't work then."

Horatio throws him a questioning look.

"We're more sensitive in what we feel – "

His voice rising in crescendo, the gravedigger bellows out the end of his song.

"'*But stealthy age with never a sound, snuck up and seized me in his clutch, and sends me back into the ground, as if this man had never been such.*'"

He finds a leg bone and some ribs, which he flings onto the dirt mound, then he brings up a second skull, this one with the top of the skeleton head missing, only the jaw bone remaining, brown earth coating the teeth and worms wriggling in the nose hole. He promptly pitches it away.

"That skull had a tongue in it at one time; it could sing," Hamlet remarks. "How he just flings it and the other parts away in disgust, like they might have been used to kill someone: a scheming politician, for all we know, who believed he would outwit God someday, but now this ass does him one better."

"It may have been so, my lord," Horatio agrees.

"Or they could have been the knees of a courtier whose life was flattery and constant bowing – 'Good morning, sweet lord. I hope you slept well, my lord.' Or the great Lord Such-and-Such, who praised Lord So-and-So's horse only because he wanted to borrow it."

"Indeed, my lord."

"And now they're at the mercy of my Lord and Lady Worm, cracked and broken, knocked on the head by a gravedigger's spade. Here's a fine turn of events if we had a mind to see it. Were these bones brought into the world just to end up being tossed about like this? I find my own aching just thinking about it."

The gravedigger begins a different song. " '*A pickaxe and a spade, a spade; the body wrapped in white. A pit of clay that's to be made, for such a guest is right.*'" He finds yet another skull, this one fully intact. He sets it at the foot of the dirt mound so it can watch him while he lies down in the grave to see how much more digging needs to be done.

"Another one – " Hamlet says, bothered. "I want to speak with this fellow." He approaches the grave and peers down at the gravedigger. "Sir, whose grave is this?"

"Mine, sir," the gravedigger replies, busy measuring the width of the grave by placing his arms at his sides and opening them. "'*Oh a pit of clay is being made –*'"

"Should I assume it's yours because you're lying in it?"

"And you're not, so it can't be yours. As for me, I'm not really lying in it, but it is mine." He gets to his feet and brushes the dirt off his clothes.

"While you were in it you were lying, because you said it was yours. But it's for the dead, not for the living. Therefore what you said was a lie."

"Ah, but it's a lively lie, sir," the gravedigger retorts jovially. "It'll jump quickly from me and *lie* with you – " he snaps his thumbs, "like that."

"Who's the man you're digging it for?"

"No man, sir."

"What woman?"

"Not a woman either."

"Who's going to be buried in it then?"

"One who was a woman, sir, but, rest her soul, now she's dead."

"How literally this rascal takes things," Hamlet remarks to Horatio, impressed with the gravedigger's verbal prowess. "He exploits the slightest ambiguity to full advantage. Do you know, I've noticed in the last few years that people have become increasingly good at this – peasant types dogging the heels of courtiers enough to be more than a little irritating." He regards the gravedigger. " – How long have you been digging graves, sir?"

"All the days of the year since the last King Hamlet defeated Fortinbras of Norway."

"How long ago was that?"

"You don't know? It was the same day young Hamlet was born – he who's gone mad and been sent to England."

"I see. And why was he sent to England?"

"I told you, because he went mad. But he'll come to his senses there. Or if he doesn't, it's neither here nor there."

"Why?"

"It won't be noticed there – the people are all as mad as he is," he laughs.

"Tell me how he came to be mad."

"Very strangely, they say."

"'Strangely'? Why is that?"

"Well, because madness is a strange thing."

"You believe so? On what grounds?"

"Danish grounds, sir! I've been caretaker of this place for thirty years," he declares proudly, "as a grown man and a boy before that."

The gravedigger's partner returns from the tavern with a bottle of ale. Fascinated by the skull sitting on the edge of the grave, Hamlet waits while the man removes the stopper and has a drink.

"How long before a buried person begins to rot, sir?"

"Well, sir," the gravedigger says, wiping a forearm across his mouth, "if they're not rotten before they die – and we've got loads of infected ones these days that barely stay in one piece till we get them buried – they may last eight or nine years. 'Course a tanner will last you the nine years."

"Why tanners more than others?"

"Well, sir, their hide is so tanned what with making leather that it keeps the water out a long time, and your water is a mean decayer of your wretched dead body." He reaches for the skull sitting on the edge of the grave. "Here's a skull been lying there twenty-three years now."

"Whose was it?"

"One ill-behaving nuisance. Whose do you think?"

"I have no idea."

"Curse him for being mad as a man can get, he poured a full jug of Rhine wine on my head once. This very skull, sir, was Yorick's skull, the old King's jester."

"This?" Hamlet takes the skull from him.

"That was he." The gravedigger takes another swig of his ale.

"Alas, poor Yorick." Hamlet studies the skull thoughtfully and turns to Horatio. "I knew him, Horatio. A wild, hilarious fellow he was – always amusing people. He let me ride on his back a thousand times, and now – how abhorrent to see such a man come to this. It's sickening. Here were the lips that kissed my cheek I don't know how often. Where are your teasing jests now, Yorick? Your comic antics, your silly songs, your merry stories that made everyone at the table roar with laughter? Your jaw gone for good, there's not even a way to laugh at yourself." He reflects somberly for a moment. "Go to my lady's bedroom and tell her she can put on make-up an inch thick, she'll still end up like this; see if I can make her laugh at that. – Horatio, tell me something."

"What's that, my lord?"

"Do you think the great Alexander looked like this in his grave?"

"I would think so."

"And smelled too?" He catches a whiff of the skull and makes a face. "Pah!" He sets it down on the side of the grave.

"And smelled too, my lord," Horatio smiles.

"To what unworthy ends we eventually come. Do you think, Horatio, that we could trace an imaginary path from the dust of noble Alexander, till we found it in the clay they use to plug holes in wine casks these days?"

"You could be stretching things a bit far to do that," Horatio suggests.

"No, not at all. Indeed, I don't think it's exaggerating to say there is some likelihood to the proposition. We know Alexander died, was buried, turned into dust, dust is earth, from earth mixed with sand we make clay mortar, and couldn't that mortar he was turned into, be filling the bung-hole in a wine cask today? Or for that matter, 'Imperial Caesar,'" he quotes from a poem, "'*dead and turned to dust, who might these days be plugging a hole to keep the wind away. Picture his dust: this man who over the world held sway, now patching a wall to keep cold gusts at bay.*' But wait – what's that – here come the King, the Queen, their courtiers – "

Coming toward them through the churchyard is a funeral procession, led by a black-robed priest. The King, the Queen, Laertes, several attendant lords and ladies, all grim-faced and dressed in dark mourning clothes, follow behind the plain pinewood coffin which six pallbearers are carrying on their shoulders. They move in solemn silence between the rows of monuments and headstones.

"Who is this they're bringing for burial?" Hamlet asks Horatio. "And with such limited ceremony. It can only mean the person ended his own life, and it was someone of considerable rank, otherwise the King and Queen wouldn't be along. Let's move over there and see what's happening – " He and Horatio slip behind a gray granite statue of a winged angel.

The pallbearers lower the coffin and set it down on the lowering straps the gravedigger and his partner have scrambled to get ready.

"What about the other half of the ceremony?" Laertes asks the priest.

"That's noble Laertes," Hamlet says uneasily.

"What about the other half of the ceremony?" Laertes asks a second time.

"The funeral rites have been in accordance with what the authorities will allow in a case like this. The manner of her death was questionable; if the King hadn't ordered us to ignore the law she would have been laid to eternal rest in unsanctified ground. Instead of prayers for grace and mercy she would have had pottery shards, stones and gravel thrown on her coffin, yet here she is, permitted to have virginal flower wreathes and funeral garlands strewn about the grave, and given holy burial with the bell tolling."

"Can nothing more be done?"

"I'm afraid not. We would be violating a most sacred precept if we sang a mourning requiem and put her to rest like someone who had died in peace."

"Lay her in the earth then, and from her fair and pristine flesh may violets spring. As for you, obstinate priest, my sister will be one of heavens' ministering angels when you lie suffering in hell."

Offended by the blasphemy, the priest casts his eyes toward the King in a look of appeal. But Claudius only shakes his head as if to say 'let him be.'

"What, the fair Ophelia?" Hamlet says out loud and steps from behind the statue, Horatio taking him by an arm to keep him back.

"Sweets for the sweet," the Queen laments, scattering blue, yellow and white flowers over Ophelia's coffin as the gravedigger and his partner lower it into the ground. "Farewell, my dear. I hoped you could have been my Hamlet's bride – I thought I would be decorating your wedding bed with flowers, sweet girl, not tossing them into your grave."

"Let worse sorrows fall," Laertes cries as he leaps into the grave, "on the vile head of the man who stripped you of your reason. Hold off shoveling the earth until I take her in my arms one more time." He drapes himself over the coffin, putting his head down on the wood. "Now pile your soil upon the living and the dead until you've turned this even ground into a mountain higher than Pelion where the Greeks climbed trying to reach the top of blue-peaked Olympus."

"What man is this whose grief pours out with such despair, whose words of sorrow grip the very stars, striking them motionless in awe? It is I, Hamlet the Dane."

Hamlet charges the grave where Laertes is up, out and throwing himself at Hamlet in a fury, the two of them grappling violently.

"The devil take your soul," Laertes cries.

"That's a sorry prayer – " Hamlet chokes, " – take your fingers from my throat – for though I'm not a man to rage, I do have something dangerous in me which you would be wise to fear. Take your hands away!"

"Break them up," the King commands.

"Hamlet!" the Queen cries as she tries to intervene. "Hamlet!" The King keeps her back while the pallbearers, Horatio and several of the lords pull Hamlet and Laertes away from each other.

"Calm down, my lord," Horatio says forcefully.

"Not even – I'll fight him till it's my last gasp."

"Over what, my son?" the Queen sobs through her tears. "Fight him over what?"

"I loved Ophelia. Forty thousand brothers all together couldn't have loved her as I did. What would you do for her?" Hamlet demands.

"He is mad, Laertes," the King says.

"For the love of God don't listen to him," the Queen pleads.

"I asked what you would do for her," Hamlet says, glaring at Laertes. "Would you weep for her, Laertes? Fight to the death for her? Starve yourself, wound yourself, take poison, eat crocodile? Because I would. Did you come here to show how you can whine, to prove something about your love by leaping into the grave? If you'll be buried alive with her, I will also. And if you want to babble about heaping mountains of earth, let them throw a million tons upon us, until a tower that would dwarf Mount Ossa burns its head on the passing sun. No, if you choose to rant and fume, I can do so just as well."

"This is madness!" the Queen says to Laertes. "He shakes in the throes of his anger when it flares, but in no time he'll sit with his head drooping silently, sorry for what he has said and done.''

"Why must you treat me like this, Laertes? You were always my friend.'' Hamlet looks into the faces of those around him, and smiles placidly. "But what does that matter now? Let Hercules himself do what he may.'' He glances at his mother. "The cat will meow,'' and then at the King, "the dog have his day.''

He breaks free of the arms that are holding him and flees.

"Go after him,'' the King says to Horatio then takes Laertes aside. "Be patient and remember what was said last night. We'll set our plan in motion soon. – Dear Gertrude, make sure your son is looked after.'' He notices the granite angel nearby. "We shall build a living likeness on this ground too. The time for peace will shortly be at hand,'' he declares hopefully. "Till then we will be patient and seek to understand…''

Hamlet and Horatio are talking with subdued voices in a window alcove across from the stairway that leads up to the castle roof.

"Enough about that, my friend. Let me get back to the other business. You remember how I described the situation I found myself in on the ship?''

"Remember it, my lord!'' Horatio exclaims.

"Lying in my cabin berth there was such a restlessness inside me I couldn't sleep. I felt I had been locked up and shackled to the floor like some mutineer. On an impulse – and praised be impulsiveness for helping us know when our carefully devised schemes have come to nothing, for having us understand there's a divinity, an over-seeing power that directs our human lives, despite the effort we put forth to further things ourselves.''

"That is quite true, my lord.''

"I jumped into my sea clothes, snuck out of my cabin and went groping in the dark to find Rosencrantz and Guildenstern. When I did, I stole their parcel of documents and went back to my cabin. Suspicion forcing me to break protocol, I boldly opened their letters from the

King, only to find a plot that would dispose of me, Horatio – an explicit order padded with all sorts of references to the King of Denmark's health, and England's too, warning of phantom ghosts and goblins that would descend like a plague if I were allowed to remain alive. The letter once read – no time even for sharpening the executioner's axe – my head was to come off in England."

"Unbelievable, my lord!"

"Here is the letter." Hamlet hands it to Horatio. "You may read it at your leisure. In the meantime, are you curious as to what I did then?"

"Very, my lord.."

"Caught in the web of his treachery – unwittingly, since the plot was underway before I realized it revolved around me – I sat and wrote out fresh orders, couching them, down to the smallest detail, in the same language the King had used. Can you guess the gist?"

"I have an idea…"

"Words of earnest appeal from his Danish Majesty, requesting that, as England was beholden to Denmark through treaty obligations; and as the love between the two nations should flourish like the placid palm tree; as the very olive branch of peace united them in harmonious friendship – and with various other significant "as'es" thrown in for good measure – he should fulfill his duties as King of England and have those who put this letter into his possession done away with immediately, denying them the opportunity to make their final confession, or seek forgiveness of their sins."

"How did you seal the new document?"

"Why, even in *that* heaven was on my side. I had my father's signet ring in my bag, which is a copy of the Danish seal. I folded my letter to look exactly like the other, signed the King's name, sealed the wax with my ring and put it back safely with no one the wiser. The next day was our fight at sea and what happened after that you already know."

"So Guildenstern and Rosencrantz face impending death?" Horatio asks with a troubled frown.

"They brought it on themselves, Horatio," Hamlet protests, "kissing up to the King as they did. They're not on my conscience. Meddling in the affairs of others was their undoing – it's a risk the uninitiated take when they step between the thrusting swords of two fierce adversaries."

"But what kingly behavior is this, my lord," Horatio wonders.

"I have no choice now, Horatio – he has killed a King, my father, made a whore of my mother, slipped in between the crown and my rightful claim to it, thrown out ever more murderous lies to lure me into his clutches – isn't it right for me to stand up against injustice, to pay him back for these things that he's done? Won't I be damned if I let this canker grow and continue to spread, rather than bring an end to what has so infected us?"

Horatio is silent for a moment.

"Word will come from England soon about what's taken place," he reminds Hamlet.

Hamlet nods. "Soon, indeed..." he says absently. "But that is more than enough time; after all, a man's whole life passes in the time it takes to count to 'one'..."

Horatio meets Hamlet's eyes and then looks away.

"But I am sorry, good Horatio, that I took out so much on Laertes, for in his cause I see my own. I'll work to stay on his good side after this, but it was the boasting about his grief that pricked my anger – "

Horatio puts a finger to his lips. "Someone's coming," he tells Hamlet.

Osric, a courtier close to the King, is relieved to have found the Prince. A young man of slight build, whose features are rustic and plain, he hurries over and curtsies more than bows to Hamlet, removing his feather-plumed hat with one hand while making elaborate, flourishing gestures with the other.

"Your Lordship is very welcome back in Denmark."

"Much thanks, sir." He looks Osric over: the fashionable clothes, the affected manner, and casts Horatio a look. "Do you know this water-fly?"

"No, my lord, I don't."

"That's a blessing, for it's something I wouldn't wish on you. He owns a great deal of fertile farmland. I guess that's what happens if you put one animal in charge of the others – he gets to have his meals with the farmer, who in this case is our King. He's of no consequence, except, as I say, that he's one of our more prominent dirt owners."

"Sweet lord, if your lordship would vouchsafe me – "

Hamlet mouths 'vouchsafe me' and winks at Horatio.

Osric sees they're making fun. "If you would give me a moment of your time, I can happily impart a thing or two from his Majesty himself."

"I will receive that thing or two, sir, with due diligence my-self. But for goodness sake, a hat is for one's head, sir." Hamlet motions him to put his on.

"I realize that, your lordship," he explains, turning the hat nervously in his hands. "but it is very hot."

"No, believe me, it is very cold; the wind is coming from the north."

"It *is* somewhat cold, my lord, indeed," he nods politely.

"And yet I *do* feel it's quite muggy and a little too warm for my liking, on the whole."

"Absolutely, my lord, it is *quite* muggy – as if it were – " he ventures, turning over phrases in his head. "Well, I can't exactly say what. But my lord," he changes topics, "his Majesty asked me to let you know that he has placed a sizeable wager on you. The details are these – "

Hamlet points to the hat, then Osric's head.

"No, please my lord, if you'd bear with me," he says, growing flustered. When he regains his composure he presses on. "Sir, Laertes has recently returned to court – and believe me when I say that he's an absolute gentleman, replete not only in his most excellent qualities and sociable disposition, but most distinguished in his appearance also. It barely does justice to him to declaim that he's the epitome of good breeding, and that in him all the attributes you could ever aspire to find in the most admirable specimen of a man, are present."

Snickering at Osric's overblown oration, Hamlet waits to see if he's finished before responding. "Sir," he begins after reflecting a moment, "his perfections certainly suffer neither diminution nor detraction in your delineation of them, though I know to make a more extensive inventory would plunge us into a mathematical morass which is bound to leave the memory reeling, and notwithstanding the fact that any attempt to further particularize his assets couldn't help but come across as prolix and cumbersome since, indigenously speaking, what he is leaves any descriptive account far behind – as a sleek vessel like his reaches fast toward the horizon while our stout yawl lags well back and drifts haplessly off course – but, not wanting to eschew verity in extolling a man so unexceptionable either, I can tell you I take him to be the genuine article, one infused with values of such estimable worth and rarity as to render words useless in particularizing them – nothing can compare with him except perhaps his own reflection; anyone who would want to emulate him couldn't help but be a pale shadow of the man."

Hamlet's tongue-in-cheek answer having gone over his hatless head for the most part, Osric can only nod and reply: "Your lordship speaks most accurately of him."

"But what's the point here, sir? Why is this man having hyperbole heaped upon him in such an unctuous and unrefined way?

"Sir?" Osric asks, bewildered.

"Can't you bring yourself to use plainer language?" Horatio pipes up. "Surely you can, sir."

"And why are we talking about Laertes in the first place?"

"Laertes?" Osric is puzzled.

"His wallet is empty," Horatio teases. "He's run out of expensive words."

"Why Laertes?" Hamlet asks again.

"I know you're not ignorant – " Osric sputters.

"I wish you *did* know that, sir. Yet I imagine if you did, it wouldn't do me much good, would it?"

Baffled, Osric can only look from Hamlet to Horatio and back again. "You are not ignorant of Laertes's excellence – "

"I would not dare to admit as much, lest you think I give a similar excellence to myself; which is presumptuous, of course, saying one knows another without really knowing oneself."

"I mean his excellence with a weapon," Osric says frostily. When neither Hamlet nor Horatio say anything, he carries on. "Among those who know the sport of fencing, he's regarded as the acme and very best there is."

Hamlet and Horatio exchange smirks.

"With what weapon is he both 'the acme and very best there is'?"

"With rapier and dagger."

"That's two weapons, isn't it?"

Osric frowns.

"Never mind…"

"The King, sir," Osric launches in, "has bet Laertes six Barbary horses and in turn Laertes has ventured, as I understand it, six of the finest French rapiers and daggers as well as the gear that goes with them – belts, straps, braces, and so on. As a matter of fact three of the carriages are impeccably designed, very adeptly fitted to the hilts – intricate workmanship, elaborately designed, as I say."

"What do you mean by the 'carriages'?"

"I knew you'd need footnotes before you were through," Horatio quips.

"The carriages, sir, are what you hold them with."

"The term would work better if we had battlefield cannons strapped around our waists. Until then I prefer 'handles'. But go on. Six Barbary horses against six French swords, all the accessories, and three most finely wrought carriages – that's what the French are betting against the Danish? – Though why are these things being "ventured" at all, as you put it?"

"The King has made a bet, sir, that in a dozen rounds between you and Laertes, he won't score enough hits to win more than two or three. For his part, Laertes gives the same odds, but against you not making enough hits. And the match can begin immediately if your Lordship would vouchsafe me an answer."

"What if my 'vouchsafed' answer is 'no'?"

"By 'answer', my lord, I mean accepting the challenge as delivered."

"Sir, I will stroll over to the hall where I often go to exercise at this time of day. You can let his Majesty know that, if the equipment is brought, the gentleman willing and the King still intent on pitting the two of us against each other, I will win for him if I can. If not, a slight embarrassment and the odd hit won't do me any harm."

"Is this what I shall say you said?"

"Something to that effect, sir – with whatever artful flourishes of hat or hand you wish to add."

"I commend my duty to your Lordship," Osric says.

Hamlet dismisses him with a curt wave but not before the spry young courtier gets in some vigorous arm movements, which Hamlet mockingly mimics.

"Yours, yours…" he says and turns to Horatio. "He does well to commend himself since no one else is likely to."

"Our little bird left the nest with bits of shell still on his head," Horatio says, poking fun.

"He probably asked his mother's permission before sucking at the nipple – like all the others in that crowd of his which I know people so frivolously idolize these days – decked out in all the latest fashions, they get catch-phrase compliments and the argot of flattering address down pat, a kind of airy, inflated vocabulary which floats them along in the presence of profound and genuinely held opinions, yet when you test them with the simplest question their bubbles burst, leaving them quite deflated and speechless."

No sooner has he finished speaking than a silver-haired Lord from the King's personal entourage presents himself.

"My lord," he begins graciously, "his Majesty conveyed a message to you through young Osric, who brought word that you are awaiting him in the hall. He would like to know if you are ready to begin with Laertes, or if you would prefer to wait a bit."

"My intentions remain unchanged," Hamlet replies. "I am happy to comply with the King's desires. If he's ready, I am too. Now or whenever, provided I can fight dressed like this." He indicates the regular clothes he is wearing.

"The King, the Queen and their retinue are coming down as we speak."

"What good timing," Hamlet remarks with thinly veiled sarcasm.

"The Queen hopes you will be civil with Laertes, treating him courteously before the bout begins."

"It's good of her to remind me…"

When the Lord has bowed and departed, Horatio comes to Hamlet's side, a grave look on his face.

"You will lose, my lord."

"No, Horatio. While he's been in France I've been practicing daily. I can beat their odds."

But something in his friend's expression touches off Hamlet's introspection.

"You wouldn't think there was a sense of foreboding in my heart right now, would you…"

"But I would, my lord."

"It's just nonsense – the misgiving of old wives. It doesn't mean anything."

"If your mind dislikes something about this, you must obey it. I will stop them on the way and say you're not well."

"Absolutely not. I put no stock in superstition: destiny is at work even in the death of a sparrow, Horatio. If my time has come, I no longer have to wait for it. If I no longer have to wait for it, my time has come. If my time has not come, then I can only continue to wait for it. The readiness is what matters. Since no man knows what his future holds, why should he care about leaving this life before he discovers what is to be?"

To a fanfare of trumpets and kettle-drums, soldiers, guards and royal attendants enter the hall and waste no time setting up tables, chairs, and cushions for the upcoming fencing match, setting out food and drink for the King, Queen, Laertes, Osric and a crowd of courtly spectators who take their places around the room a few moments later. As Osric arranges the fencing foils and daggers on a royal blue-and-gold cushion, the King holds Laertes's hand in the air.

"Come, Hamlet! Come and take this hand."

Hamlet goes over and shakes with Laertes.

"I offer you my apologies, sir. I have done you wrong. But I hope, as you are a gentleman, you will allow me to make amends. Those gathered here know, and you must have heard, how I am suffering from a debilitating malady of the mind. Whatever I have done to offend your sense of honor, to distract you from your duty as a son and brother, and to provoke you personally, I can assure you was the result of this affliction. Was it Hamlet who wronged Laertes? Never. If Hamlet is somehow severed from himself, and that part wrongs

Laertes, then Hamlet denies he is at fault. But who is? The madness. Which means that Hamlet is also of that party that has been wronged; his madness is the unfortunate Hamlet's enemy as well. Sir, before this audience here assembled, let me again deny any harm I have done to you. Free me of the charge that it was intentional, as you would if I shot an arrow over the house and injured my brother."

"I am satisfied in my duty as a son, which in this case would be what stirs me most to have revenge. But where honor is concerned, I remain undecided and won't be reconciled till those with wisdom and experience in such matters advise me how I should make peace with you and still preserve my reputation. For the time being I accept your offer of friendship as friendship alone, and will in all ways respect it."

"I welcome it happily and will play out this brotherly wager without rancor. Give us the foils."

"Come, one for me," Laertes calls and waves Osric over with the cushion on which numerous foils are displayed. He inspects the weapons carefully.

"I'll be your foil, Laertes," Hamlet offers. "Against my lack of experience your skill will stand out like a star in the darkest night."

"Don't mock me, sir," Laertes replies with a jovial smile.

"I'm not, upon my word."

"See to their foils, young Osric," the King says, catching Laertes's eye as a hint to select his weapon.

"Cousin Hamlet, you know the wager?"

"Quite well, my lord. Your Grace has bet on the weaker side."

"I'm not worried," the King replies, watching Laertes out of the corner of his eye. "I have seen both of you, but since he's that much better we've adjusted the odds accordingly."

Hamlet picks up a foil and tries it out.

After some practice swipes and thrusts, Laertes puts his foil back on Osric's cushion.

"This one is too heavy. Let me have another."

"I like this one," Hamlet declares, appraising his weapon then peering across at the new foil Laertes has selected. "Are they all the same length?"

"Yes, my good lord," Osric assures him, turning away quickly.

As the fencers take their positions, servants circulate among the spectators pouring wine from silver flagons.

"Set it over here when the cups are filled," the King orders. "If Hamlet makes the first or second hit, or if he and Laertes both exchange hits in the third round, let the cannons fire from the ramparts. The King shall toast Hamlet's impressive performance and drop a pearl into his cup more valuable than those which four successive Kings have worn in their crowns – bring me the cups – let the kettle-drum signal to the trumpet, the trumpet alert the cannoneer on the parapet, the cannons then sound to the heavens and heaven announce to earth, that 'Now the King drinks to Hamlet.' Come, begin, and you our judges watch the proceedings carefully."

"Come on, sir," Hamlet says, cutting the air with his foil as a salute to his opponent.

"Ready, my lord," Laertes replies, takes his position, returns Hamlet's salute and meets him in a flurry of clashing metal.

"One!" Hamlet calls after a minute.

"No," Laertes objects.

"Judgement?"

Osric steps forward. "A hit, a very palpable hit!" he announces.

"Wait while I drink," the King says, Osric quickly stepping between the fencers and motioning them to remain apart. The King holds up his right hand for all to see. "Hamlet, this pearl, is yours." He slips the ring from his finger and drops it into the silver wine cup on the table beside him, no one noticing that he has flipped up the large pearl atop the ring, releasing a dose of poison into the wine. "Here's to your health!" he says, toasting Hamlet. He takes the cup sitting next to the one in which he has just deposited the pearl ring, and drinks. Almost immediately, kettledrums begin to roll on the other side of the room, a bright trumpet fanfare follows, and a moment later cannon fire thunders outside the castle. "Give him his cup," the King says, hoisting Hamlet's wine.

"I'll play this bout first," Hamlet says, declining. "Set it down for the time being. Come – "

He and Laertes resume fencing, Hamlet striking him once more on the right arm.

"Another hit?"

"Laertes offers a frustrated nod. "I would say so.""

"It seems our son will win," the King remarks to Gertrude.

"He's perspiring and very short of breath. Here, Hamlet, take my handkerchief and dry your face. The Queen drinks to your good fortune!"

"Much thanks, madam," Hamlet says, unaware that his mother is putting his cup of wine up to her lips.

"Gertrude, don't drink," the King says sternly.

"I will, my lord," the Queen insists, "excuse me."

She sips some wine and holds the cup out to Hamlet.

"The poisoned cup, but it's too late – " the King says under his breath.

"Not yet, mother."

"At least let me wipe your face, then." She sets the wine down and pulls a handkerchief from the sleeve of her dress.

"My lord," Laertes calls to the King in a hushed whisper, "I'll hit him now – "

"I can't say – " the King mutters, his eyes on Gertrude.

" – though it almost goes against my conscience," Laertes says to himself.

"The next bout, Laertes," Hamlet says, buoyed by his success thus far. "Come on, no more stalling – and give it your best this time – so far you've only been toying with me."

"You think so? Come on, then."

Osric has them take positions and then gives the signal to commence.

They parry and thrust back and forth inconclusively, the intensity mounting on both sides, until Hamlet lunges and almost scores a hit; Laertes does the same a moment later.

"Nothing either way!" Osric shouts.

"See about this," Laertes warns and lunges violently with his poisoned rapier, wounding Hamlet. His shoulder bleeding, Hamlet fights back with an aggressiveness Laertes is unprepared for, beating his opponent's foil down and batting it out of his hand in a wild, ruthless swipe. Without a weapon now, Laertes hurls himself at Hamlet, who drops his sword and holds up his arms to defend himself, but Laertes is too fast – he throws Hamlet to the ground and picks up the dropped sword, but Hamlet has grabbed the foil Laertes was using and got back on his feet.

"Separate them or they'll kill each other!" the King cries.

"Come again," Hamlet shouts defiantly and as they clash once more, Hamlet manages to hit Laertes in the ribs when he fails to dodge the poisoned foil.

"Something's happened to the Queen – " Osric cries in alarm.

Watching the fencers, Horatio has quickly become distressed. "They're bleeding badly," he tells the others and hurries to Hamlet's side. "How are you, my lord?"

"Are you hurt?" Osric demands and rushes to help Laertes, whose wound is severe.

"Caught like a fool in my own trap – " Laertes groans, wincing as his pain worsens. "Justly killed through my own treachery, Osric."

"How is the Queen?" Hamlet cries, Horatio helping him make his way over to Gertrude, lying on the floor with her head propped up by the cushion on which the foils were displayed..

"She's feinted from the sight of all this blood," the King declares.

"No – " the Queen gasps, surrounded by servants and numerous lords. "The drink – O my dear Hamlet! I've been poisoned – " She raises her head bravely to see where Hamlet is, but weakens and lets herself be lowered to the cushion, where she dies...

"O villainy! Listen all – " Hamlet shrieks. "Lock the doors! Find out whose treachery this is!"

Osric appeals for help with Laertes and sees that he's gently laid down before rushing from the room, presumably to carry out Hamlet's orders.

"It was my doing, Hamlet," Laertes says, struggling to speak. "The wound I gave you is fatal – No medicine in the world can help you now. There's not half an hour's life left – and the deadly weapon is in your hand, no blunt cap on the point, dabbed in poison. How this heinous plot has turned against me. Look where I now end off, never to rise again. Your mother – poisoned as well. It's over. The King, Hamlet – the King's to blame."

"The point wet with poison too?" Hamlet cries. "Then venom, do your duty – " he shouts, and charges the King, horrified screams of "Treason!" filling the room as Hamlet plunges his sword into Claudius.

"Some of you – defend me!" he shouts an appeal to his subjects, "I am only wounded – "

Throwing down his foil, Hamlet plucks the poisoned cup of wine. "Here, you incestuous, murderous, damned Dane – finish drinking the rest of your concoction!" Seizing Claudius by the throat he forces the wine into his mouth. "Is your pearl here?" he demands when he is done, flinging Claudius to the floor beside Gertrude. "Join her!" His body convulsing violently, Claudius begins choking and dies a moment later with a piteous groan.

Laertes, clinging to life, sees Hamlet standing over the dead King and Queen.

"He has tasted his own medicine at last – it was a poison he mixed himself, Hamlet. Let us forgive each other, noble friend. You can't be blamed for my death or my father's, nor I for yours."

On the brink of collapse, Hamlet takes a few steps but staggers badly and is about to fall, when Horatio reaches out and steadies him.

"Heaven acquit you for it," Hamlet murmurs quietly, the color draining from his face as he realizes Laertes is dead. "I follow him, Horatio." He turns and glances back at his mother's body. "My poor Queen, farewell." He takes in the shocked faces of those watching, stares vacantly ahead before speaking. "You who look pale and tremble as you gaze upon such misfortune – " He looks down at his blood-soaked white shirt, and over at Laertes's bloodied clothes. "Silent witnesses to what has here taken place, had I the time – but, you see, this cruel sergeant Death presses forward with his arrest – O, I could tell you much – but, let it be." He slumps in Horatio's arms. "Horatio, I am dead, but you live on. Let any who have not heard… know the truth about me and what, in my way, I tried to do."

"That will never be," Horatio declares. "I am more an ancient Roman than a Dane – there's still some drink left in the cup. Give me death before dishonor – " Overcome with emotion, he picks up the wine cup and futilely tries to drink from it, Hamlet using his remaining strength to wrest the vessel from him.

"Horatio – "

They struggle briefly, but when Horatio realizes what he's doing, he puts his arms around Hamlet and embraces him gratefully.

"I leave behind a tarnished name, Horatio. There is so much that will never be known – " He pauses. "If ever you had the least affection for me – put aside your own happiness for awhile and in these cruel times, painful though it may be, see that my story gets told – "

A fife and drum can be heard not far off, followed by the sound of soldiers marching and the crack of cannon salvos.

"The sound of war…" Hamlet whispers in a weakened voice as Horatio lies him gently down, just before Osric comes running into the hall.

"Young Fortinbras," Osric announces, "triumphant over Poland, fires his guns in honor of the newly arrived ambassadors from England."

His strength waning fast, Hamlet searches but can't find the locket with his father's picture that he wears around his neck. Horatio sees the problem, reaches behind for the locket and undoes the clasp. He puts it in Hamlet's hand and closes his fingers.

"I die, Horatio. The potent poison triumphs against my spirit. I won't live to hear the news from England, but I predict Fortinbras will win the nation's favor. He has my dying wish. Let him know that, and from your lips recount events both great and small which brought us to this pass – the rest is silence…"

A serene, almost contented expression comes into his face, and he dies. A grim silence descends upon the hall, all eyes turning to Horatio.

"Now breaks a noble heart," he says gazing down at Hamlet. "Good night, sweet Prince, and flights of angels sing thee to thy rest…"

Drums and the sounds of marching soldiers can be heard not far away. Those gathered in the hall shift restlessly on their feet. Uncertain as to what should be done next, they continue to watch Horatio.

"Why does the drum draw near?" he asks and listens as its beat grows louder.

Fortinbras shortly marches into the hall and his armored troops fan out around the room, a platoon of guards escorting the English ambassadors forward to stand with him taking in the sad spectacle.

"What is this my eyes behold?" Fortinbras asks in dismay.

"What is it you wish to see?" Horatio replies. "If something steeped in tragedy and sorrow, look no further."

"These lifeless, bloody bodies speak of dangerous slaughter. O Death what feast have you prepared in your eternal dwelling place that takes so many noble lives in one fell swoop?"

"This is a most dismal sight," one of the English ambassadors offers. "Our news from England comes too late. The ears that would hear us tell him his order has been carried out – Rosencrantz and Guildenstern are dead – beyond listening now, and none to offer us thanks...

"Not his mouth, had it the ability to speak; he never did command their deaths. But to deal with this bloody business before us – since you, Fortinbras, have returned from your Polish campaign, and you, ambassadors from England, are present, lend your authority and give direction for these bodies to lie in a place of honor for the world to view, allowing me to address those still uninformed so I might explain how these things came about. In so doing I will talk of carnal, cruel and bloody acts, of vengeance gone awry, of accidental slaughter, of deaths by cunning and conspiring, and, through this, of schemes that were foiled and turned about, hurting those who had put them into play. All this I can honestly relate."

"Let us gather the noblest peers quickly," Fortinbras declares, "so they can have benefit of hearing. As for me, I embrace my good fortune, however sadly. I have historic rights within this realm, which now I have the opportunity to claim."

"Of that I will also want to speak," Horatio tells him. "Words from the mouth of him whose voice can no more be heard. And let this be done immediately – though much is yet unsettled – before something worse befalls the state on top of these misfortunes."

Fortinbras acknowledges Horatio solemnly, then turns to gaze on Hamlet.

"Four captains shall bear the Prince like a soldier to the hallowed place where all may render their respect, for had he assumed his rightful role he would have proved himself most royal; at his burial the fallen soldier's dirge shall play, and cannons from the battlements salute his passing. Remove the bodies. Such a sight as this belongs to a field of battle, but here is sorely out of place. Go, bid the cannons fire."

Soldiers drape the bodies and shoulder them for carrying. When all are ready, the procession files gravely through the great hall as the guns of Elsinore begin to thunder, saluting Hamlet, Prince of Denmark....

The Shakespeare Novels

Spring 2006

Hamlet
King Lear
Macbeth
Midsummer Night's Dream
Othello
Romeo and Juliet
Twelfth Night

Spring 2007

As You Like It
The Merchant of Venice
Measure for Measure
Much Ado About Nothing
The Taming of the Shrew
The Tempest

www.crebermonde.com

Shakespeare Graphic Novels

Fall 2006

Hamlet
Macbeth
Othello
Romeo and Juliet

www.shakespearegraphic.com

New Directions

The Young and the Restless: *Change*
The Human Season: *Time and Nature*
Eyes Wide Shut: *Vision and Blindness*
Cosmos: *The Light and The Dark*
Nothing But: *The Truth in Shakespeare*
Relationscripts: *Characters as People*
Idol Gossip: *Rumours and Realities*
Wherefore?? *The Why in Shakespeare*
Upstage, Downstage: *The Play's the Thing*
Being There: *Exteriors and Interiors*
Dangerous Liaisons: *Love, Lust and Passion*
Iambic Rap: *Shakespeare's Words*
P.D.Q.: *Problems, Decisions, Quandaries*
Antic Dispositions: *Roles and Masks*
The View From Here: *Public vs. Private Parts*
3D: *Dreams, Destiny, Desires*
Mind Games: *The Social Seen*
Vox: *The Voice of Reason*

Paul Illidge is a novelist and screenwriter who taught high school English for many years. He is the creator of *Shakespeare Manga*, the plays in graphic novel format, and author of the forthcoming *Shakespeare and I*. He is currently working on *Shakespeare in America*, a feature-film documentary. Paul Illidge lives with his three children beside the Rouge River in eastern Toronto.